THE WHITE STREAK

OTHER TITLES BY MAX BRAND:

Rusty Sabin (2014)
Valley of Outlaws (2014)
The Sacred Valley (2014)
Peyton (2015)
The Steel Box (2015)
Red Fire (2015)
Jingo (2017)
The Winged Horse (2017)
Curry (2017)
The Western Double (2017)
Daring Duval (2017)
Bandit's Trail (2018)
Old Carver Ranch (2018)
The Brass Man (2018)
Saddlemates (2018)
The Trail Beyond (2018)
Sour Creek Valley (2018)
Sunset Wins (2018)
The Cure of Silver Cañon (2018)
Torturous Trek (2018)
Jigger Bunts (2019)
Magic Gun (2019)
Luck and a Horse (2020)

THE WHITE STREAK

A Western Duo

Max Brand®

**BLACK
STONE**
PUBLISHING

Printed in the United States of America

ISBN 978-1-0940-8639-2
Fiction / Westerns

Version 1

CIP data for this book is available
from the Library of Congress

Blackstone Publishing
31 Mistletoe Rd.
Ashland, OR 97520

www.BlackstonePublishing.com

CONTENTS

THE WHITE STREAK

I

It is the instinct of Nordic humanity, since the days of John Calvin, that man must be rewarded for suffering on earth. The Deity becomes a sort of divine bookkeeper whose balance must always strike at the end, and therefore the man who has harvested pleasures on this earth cannot reasonably complain if he finds that he is facing a debit hereafter. By the same token, he who lives in misery may expect a reward. Something is coming to him, and come it must!

For this reason young Jimmy Babcock approached the office of the bank president with a perfect surety and a peace of mind. For two years he had been engaged to Muriel Aiken; for two years he had walked the cold corridors of the Merchant's Bank; for two years he had endured pain. It was true that he expected to marry Muriel a little later—with his next promotion—but that was only a partial reward for what he had endured. As he stood in the outer room, waiting to be called to the great man at the latter's pleasure, he heard the shrill, yipping voices of schoolboys playing in the vacant lot, and he stepped to the window to watch. There were a dozen of them with half of a stuffed sack for a football and the true fury of gridiron warriors in their hearts.

Jimmy Babcock smiled and nodded at the sight of them. On that same vacant lot, he once had been a hero, had run touchdowns, smashed lines, and punched noses at need. But he had gone on to greater things. On the high school team, he had raced to many a victory; he had become a triple-threat man; he could run ends of smash lines; he could pass uncanny distances and make the ball float down as of its own birdlike volition to the receiver's arms; and also he had what the news-paper reporters referred to as an "inspired toe."

As a result of that, when he finished his high school course two years before, Jimmy was not unnoticed. Six great universities told him that their front doors were trembling with eagerness to receive him. That is to say, the universities themselves did not say so, because of course that encourages professionalism. But elderly graduates dropped in to see Jimmy as he was working in his father's laundry that summer, and they made suggestions. It appeared that they had a paternal inter-est in his welfare. They had heard of him, and that he was an upstanding youth without the necessary means to go to univer-sity. Each, in turn, would be glad to finance Jimmy for four long years, but only if he would go to a certain college, and if, while there, he saw fit to turn out and join the football squad.

Jimmy, listening, had grinned horribly, as with a devouring hunger, because he knew exactly what would happen if he went on to one of the upper institutions of learning. He knew, his playmates guessed it, his high school coach was certain. There was Red Brennan, last year's halfback, who had gone east and was starring for the Red. Well, what was Brennan? An ice wagon, compared with Jimmy Babcock. And there was Arrowdale's splendid star of two years back who was now making glorious history in the Last for the Blue! Well, what of Arrowdale's Man of Mystery when Jimmy Babcock had played against him?

No, he knew beyond the mere deeds in his record. He knew by the pride of his muscles and the fury of his heart that to him all football lines would be as waving reeds, to be slipped through, or rudely broken and trampled underfoot! He had not yearned to go to college for the sake of greater learning, because he was not an ounce a student. But with a mighty yearning, his soul had stretched out its hands for the glory that was his for the taking. His deeds in Dresser High School might ring through the county. His deeds for the Blue, his chosen Holy Land, would have rung through the wide United States. He would have become a famous man, his actions, his words, his very thoughts occupying more space in the public print than those of the president of our land.

But he was nineteen. Muriel Aiken was seventeen. And even if he were willing to wait until the end of four long college years, something told him that she would not. She would have the best heart in the world, and the strongest will. But where there is honey, the bees will eat!

She was too pretty, too happy, too friendly—and too independent—to remain alone in life. And so one day, while he was driving his father's laundry wagon, and balancing in his mind the Red on the one hand and the Blue on the other, and wondering whether he would go out for the squad of ends or for halfback—at that moment he had looked up from a dream and seen Muriel Aiken walking racket in hand toward the tennis courts and a handsome blond youth beside her. And he had seen how womanhood was swelling in the body of Muriel and shining from her eyes.

That evening he dressed in his best and stood nervously before the mirror, wishing that his ears did not stick out so far and that his nose had not been peeled by the fierce summer sun. Then he went to call on Muriel and told her with a trembling voice that he not only loved her and intended to marry her but he was going to sacrifice his career to do so. That evening, Muriel, overcome, said no, and meant yes.

Then a religious enthusiasm filled the heart of Jimmy Babcock. He became pure of poker and late hours. Once a week he saw Muriel Aiken. And every day he labored hard and long in the bank.

He hated figures and figuring. They swam and whirled before his eyes. His very stomach writhed into a knot of horror and protest as he cast up accounts. But this was the pain he must accept in order to be happy forever. Sometimes his soul shrank as he cast his eye forward into the future, even as far forward as assistant cashier. No doubt that man was successful. But he was thirty years old.

Thirty years! Nine years between that age and the age of Jimmy Babcock! The same infinity which lay between his twelfth year and his twenty-first!

Heartsick when he considered such prospects, Jimmy Babcock would not give in. Just as he had labored in the frost of the morning and the dusk of the day learning the baffling intricacies of the forward pass until his big hands had mastered it, so now he bent himself earnestly to his labors. He never let a day go by with a single duty undone. And thrice the president, in those three years, had called him into his office, and thrice there had been an advance in pay. Oh, not a great deal, but enough to prove that the eye of the great man has seen and that it had understood.

So Jimmy Babcock, in that waiting room, held his patience and weighed the long cost before him, the long sacrifice already behind him, and said that Muriel was worth it all.

Then the door opened, and there issued a smiling borrower, and behind him William Parker, the bank president, nodded at Jimmy, and Jimmy went in.

The president usually went behind his desk at once, because the breadth of that mahogany surface was just the margin which he needed added to his dignity of age. For William Parker was only thirty-five, yet for eight years he had owned this institution, lock, stock, and barrel, and made it grow as the town of Dresser grew. Neither did he look a whit more than his age, what with his sandy hair and his pale gray eyes. But when he sat behind the authority of his desk and looked at a client as down the barrel of a rifle, his years became of little importance, and his knowledge of business, and the money in his vaults, was the one thing of importance. He had proved his prescience over and over. He it was who first had imported a geologist, paid him a fat salary, and thereby located oil. Now there were a dozen wells near Dresser. The giant skeletons of the derricks were the promise of future wealth, and young William Parker had brought this to Dresser and to the county. All he needed was the passage of years to make him a state figure. He anticipated time, somewhat, by doing nothing to prevent the falling of his hair, and by combing it so that the bald spot showed its increasing margin. He wore a closely cropped moustache and a beard trimmed to a point. Upon the street he wore a derby hat, chamois gloves, unbuttoned and loose upon his hands; he carried a brightly polished malacca stick. In these ways he built up, as one might say, a personality which was worth an extra couple of hundred thousands of capital to his bank and to his business.

On this day, however, Parker did not sit behind his desk. Instead, he walked to a window and beckoned Jimmy to his side. Standing half a pace of respect behind the great man, young Babcock noticed for the first time that, to an inch, he was the height of the great man, his shoulders of the same breadth and depth, his neck of the same round, hard make. Before, he had always thought of William Parker as a man of business. Now he realized that, with ten years knocked from his shoulders, William Parker would have been something on a football field. And the heart of Jimmy Babcock swelled with dizzy hope!

Parker was saying: "In one way, Babcock, this is a bank. In another way, it's something else. Do you guess what I mean?"

He pointed out of the window to the far-off rim of hills. To the rippling lines that descended to the plains. To the irrigation fields, softly green with alfalfa growing. To the black gibbets yonder—three of the oil derricks that belonged to William Babcock and Company.

"I don't guess what you mean," said Jimmy frankly. "Unless you mean something about the future of Dresser county, Mr. Parker?"

The other turned abruptly from the window. "I mean that this county is a living body. This bank is the heart which pumps blood through its veins. Looked at in that light, one will come to regard the bank differently. A heart has certain muscles, certain valves. Suppose that one of the muscles were inefficient, Jimmy?"

"I would go to a doctor, I suppose you mean?"

"Yes. Exactly. You'd go to a doctor if your heart didn't function right. Well, considering that this bank is the heart of the county, pumping blood through the arteries of its business . . . suppose that there is a valve in that heart not seriously out of order, but still not as good and strong as could be wished?"

Jimmy Babcock frowned in the intensity of his effort to understand this language. But his effort failed.

Parker raised a stiff forefinger and behind it his gray eyes were cold and steady, as behind an aimed gun.

"I mean you, Babcock. For two years I've watched you. I've given you promotions to encourage you. I've tried to bring the best out of you. I've hoped that you would grow and expand, just as Dresser County had changed in ten years from a cow range to oil and alfalfa country. But you're not what I want. You're a faulty muscle, a leaking valve in this heart. I'm going to discharge you this evening . . . with a month's pay in lieu of notice."

II

Jimmy Babcock went back to his desk, closed his ledger, took his hat and the folded newspaper which, carried in his hand, gave him a businesslike dignity as he walked home after work.

He was about to walk out of the cage without a word, but at the door he changed his mind. This was like running away from defeat. So at the door he turned and faced the others.

"So long, everybody," he said. "The can has been tied on me!"

Then he went away, knowing, from the corner of his eye, that heads had been nodded as though the others were not surprised.

He felt sick and a little dizzy. He was glad when he got past the front door into the street, for the sight of the blue sky was a restorative, and the noise of traffic heartened him. He was a failure.

Those others in the bank had known it long before, and that was why not a glint of surprise had appeared in their eyes but, rather, a touch of satisfaction. Not one had followed him, shaken his hand. Nobody had said: "Too bad, old fellow." Or some such words.

Not in such a manner had his teammates spoken on the

football field when he failed to make yards through the line or was thrown for a loss around the end. Then there was always a hand on his back.

"We'll split them open as wide as a barn door the next time, Jimmy! We'll send you through a mile!"

But then, that was because he had known football. The knowledge of it filled him. To the most mysterious enemy formations, he had felt the key of understanding tingling in his fingertips. One instant to dance back—then straight and true at the heart of the play, ripping the secondary defense apart, lodging his hard shoulder against the runner's thigh.

That had been his business. He knew that. But banking was quite another matter.

Well, he had failed. He set his teeth and had to draw a breath through them immediately. He could remember others who had failed. Young Josh Perkins had tried out a place in the Wilkins Syndicate and lost it after a year. Eyes had followed him around the streets; a bell seemed to toll behind him . . . failure! Who wanted young men who failed? Perkins had had to leave the town and go elsewhere to find an opening worthwhile. And yet Perkins was not a bad sort of a fellow—a little slow, but a dependable guard and a great help on a play inside tackle.

Jimmy Babcock went down the street with a smile carved upon his lips. The ice wagon went by with a red-shirted Irishman on the front seat, whistling. And with a good reason—he had not aimed too high, but had taken his proper place in the world, and accepted three meals a day and a room without misgiving.

He walked along by the vacant lot, and the shrill yells of the football players rang hollow in his ears. They might learn to be good players on that field, but they never would learn to be successful businessmen.

It was early autumn; the days were shortening, and already the western shadows covered half the streets as Jimmy Babcock began to walk across the town toward the Hill. All the best residences in Dresser were there. The Aiken house showed its brow over a screen of trees—a new forehead, brand new.

The Aikens had made a lot of money in the past four years. William Parker had showed them how to do it. That fellow . . . he could turn anything into money! So he had lifted the Aikens up there to the Hill, with the rest of the successes of Dresser. They were on the same street as the Wilkins place with its tower, and the broad rear of Parker's own house showed, masked by some thin columns of real stone.

No fake about William Parker! A man came all the way from Denver to carve the capitals. Thorough, that was what Parker was. Nothing cheap about him, no four-flushing.

A block from the Parker house stood the Club. Parker had founded that. With its founding, social distinctions really began. Before, there had been the whites and the Mexicans. Now there were the Club Members—and the rest of the town.

That was like Parker again. To his own high level he had drawn up a few of the select spirits.

At the foot of the Hill, a wind came scurrying and covered Jimmy Babcock with dust and dead leaves. He brushed them off without anger or malice, for it seemed only right that he should be overwhelmed by some sign of displeasure when he went up the road to the Hill. He came from the lower half of the city where his father owned a laundry.

The Aikens had a wrought iron gate now. They had a lawn, too. It looked a bit mangey, so far, but there was a splendid iron deer in the corner, peeping from among the shrubs, and in the center there was a fat lady in limestone, with legs like the tails of fishes. From a conch she blew forth a spray of water.

Jimmy Babcock knew nothing about art, and he always told himself that as he passed by the limestone mermaid.

The Aikens had a divided stairway to approach their front doorway, like an old French palace. And when Jimmy Babcock had climbed to the top of it and rung the bell, he had to wait a minute and look forth on the lower flats of Dresser, and across to the bars of water that appeared among the alfalfa fields in the irrigation ditches. Down there in the flat—that was where the Babcocks belonged, running laundries and things like that.

The door opened, and the face of a Negro servant appeared. The eyes wrinkled kindly at him. Jimmy Babcock went into the reception room, and presently a step rustled to the door. There was Mrs. Aiken in a dress of flowered silk. She wore gloves, too. She generally did, for time would not fade the red of her hands nor reduce the veins of labor upon their backs.

"How do you do, Jimmy?" she said. "Did you bring a message from Mr. Parker?"

Jimmy grew red, ashamed for her.

"I came up to see Muriel, if I may," he said.

"Muriel? Muriel?" said Mrs. Aiken. "I think she's busy. I'll go myself to see."

She went off. It was plain that Mrs. Aiken was not charmed to see him—she who received William Parker.

It showed Parker's heart that he had been so kind to the Aikens. He even was forcing rough John Aiken through the doors and into the Club, it was said.

Then footfalls tapped in the distance, and he heard Muriel's cheerful voice. He heard the voice of her mother, muffled, rapid. But here came Muriel, undeterred, and swept into the room.

"Why did you come in here, like a stick?" she demanded. "I

was on the tennis court with Sammy May. He gave me fifteen, but I beat him. Sammy hated it, too. Didn't you Sammy?"

Sammy came unwilling in the rear. He looked embarrassed, but he was only hot and sweating.

"She's getting a forehand," Sammy commented. "You oughta see her burn it across court. She can receive, too."

"She can, all right," said Jimmy Babcock. "She beat me last Sunday, Sammy."

"Sure. I suppose she did," Sammy said with a yawn. "I gotta be going. Goodbye, Jim. Muriel, you get a hop on your serve, and we'll play doubles at the Club when the tournament comes. Jim'll be busy at the bank."

"I won't be busy at the bank," Jimmy said, and again a smile was carved upon his lips.

"Hello! You taking a vacation at last?" asked Sammy.

"He's been working like an eight-day clock," Muriel said fondly.

"Permanent vacation," Jimmy replied. "I'm fired."

"Aw, what's the idea?" Sammy asked in disgust. "Parker wouldn't chuck you, you know."

"He means it," Muriel said suddenly. "Sammy, run along, will you?"

"Oil's better than banking anyway," Sammy opined. "So long, everybody."

He left them, and Jimmy and Muriel looked gravely at one another.

"He said I didn't have the right kind of an imagination for the banking business . . . Something about the right sort of muscles . . . a bank is a heart . . . pumps business through a country. It was over my head, Muriel. All I could understand was that I was thrown for a loss."

She hesitated. "What're you going to do?" she finally asked.

"Oh, I don't know. I've got twenty-five hundred saved up. I'll be a capitalist, maybe . . . and live on my income."

"Mother!" Muriel called from the door.

Mrs. Aiken came, serene and cold.

"William Parker has discharged Jimmy."

"Has he?" Mrs. Aiken said, and a spark appeared in her eye that was not anger.

"It's treachery. That's what it is," Muriel stated. "He was up here only last evening, talking as sweet as you please about everything. Dad will get you back into the bank, Jimmy. Don't you worry!"

"Don't say that," said Jimmy. He turned crimson, adding: "I wouldn't go back in there. Nothing could make me. I can't live on favors."

"What could have made him do it?" cried Muriel.

"My dear Muriel," Mrs. Aiken said acidly. "I suppose William Parker knows his business."

"Jimmy, what'll you do?" Muriel asked again.

"You'll give me back a ring," said Jimmy Babcock, "and I'll give you another chance. I never could make a home worthy of you, Muriel. That's plain. I . . . I'm a failure."

She stepped back from him a little. But her mother said: "Jimmy, I must say that you're showing a level head and good sense."

"Jimmy!" Muriel cried.

"A young fellow without expectations," continued Mrs. Aiken, "he don't want a girl around his neck, Muriel."

Her grammar slipped, now and then—but usually it slipped uphill. She was studying a word book.

"Humph," Muriel said. "I'd like to see you jilt me, Jimmy."

"I didn't mean . . ." he said. "I only came to let you know . . ."

"I'm going to marry you tomorrow!" Muriel stated.

"Muriel Aiken!" her mother cried. "Are you . . . I never heard of anything so ridiculous . . . such outrageous nonsense. I wish . . . I . . ."

"I'm going home with you to supper, Jimmy," said the girl. "And we'll ask your mother and father if I can marry you at once."

"Muriel, do you know what your expectations could be if . . ."

"I don't care anything about anything but Jimmy! Kiss me, darling Jimmy!"

"Muriel . . . you fool!" her mother cried out, and rushed from the room.

III

Muriel went upstairs to bathe and change.

Jimmy sat in the reception room with his folded hands crushed between his knees. He was trying to think and come to a brilliant conclusion. He was saying words over and over; he would start at anything, and he would force his way up.

But the weight of William Parker's authority lay over him like a leaden cloud and told him he was a failure. Then he turned dark with despair. There was money in the world, and if he did not have the wits, he had the hands to take it. He could shoot straight, at least. *I'll do murder for her,* said Jimmy in his tragic heart of hearts.

Then Muriel came down to him in a white dress, with white buckskin shoes, and a red scarf twisted around her throat in lieu of a wrap, and a red hat that kept a flush upon her face. She was not tall, and she wore low heels, so that Jimmy Babcock stared at her almost bitterly for a moment.

He said not a word until they were through the front door, and then he paused at the top step. "You're young, Muriel," he told her, "and you just are throwing yourself away on me. It makes my heart ache when I think of how I'd provide for you. I'd want you to live with flowers and nice things and everything right. If I weren't a low hound, I wouldn't have waited for you, just now. I would have gone away. But you're so straight and square, you're so beautiful, Muriel . . . My God, I can't say it very well."

"You think I'm afraid of work?" she asked him fiercely.

He took a gloved hand. The glove made it seem all the smaller, and the hand automatically curled around his finger.

"You, work?" he said, trembling with pity and with tenderness.

"You bet I'll work. I'll show you, Jimmy Babcock."

"Look here . . . I'll tell you what's my speed. A cowpuncher! That's about what I'm fitted for."

"I'd love it," she told him. "What do I care for putting on the dog? My dad was a cowpuncher. You think I'm ashamed of him? I'll tell a man that I'm not. You come along. You'll have me crying in a minute. I'm not marrying your work. I'm marrying you!"

He went unsteadily down the steps with her, his lips twitching, his eyes dim. He had the same frightful impulse to cry that he had had when he was a boy in the midst of a fistfight, or later on the football field. He never had given way; he did not give way now.

The door jerked open above them, and Mrs. Aiken's voice screamed after them like the scream of a hawk: "Muriel! You know what you're doing? You gonna go away like this with no chaperone? Without nothin'? You gonna drag yourself in the dirt? You gonna make yourself town talk?"

"I hope the town does talk," Muriel called back, hardly turning toward her mother.

"Muriel!" She choked with despair. "I tell you, you're

throwing away your opportunities! Muriel, will you come back and please let me talk to you for one minute?"

"You'd better go back to her," said Jimmy Babcock.

"Come along," she responded, and dragged him forward. The door crashed like an imprecation behind them.

"Please go back, Muriel," Jimmy pleaded. "It'll break up your home. She'll never want to see you . . ."

"Be still," Muriel said firmly. "It's a funny thing how it makes a man nervous, when a few words fly around. They're not dishes. They won't break."

"You're giving up everything for me," Jimmy said.

"I'm getting the whole of everything best in the world in exchange," she said. "And Dad will understand . . . bless him."

"I won't have his help," Jimmy told her.

"You bet you won't," said his lady. "We'll take nothing. We'll fight it out together. Oh, I can't wait!"

He looked down to the ground, and he watched the springing tread of the girl, and the low, broad heels, and the square-made toes of her shoes. Such is the strange nature of man, that from the contemplation of her shoes, his love turned to worship. His heart ached with great throbbing pangs of joy, and he went on silently beside her.

Through the rose-and-golden evening they went across the town. They left the pavements, and they passed onto a board-walk along a street where the wagon track twisted back and forth following the winter ruts. A delivery cart jangled in the distance and tufts of acrid dust shone in the air.

Then they came to a cottage whose front was embow-ered in cataracts and falls of honeysuckle. John Babcock was watering the front lawn. He was wearing overalls over his trousers, and he heeded not the fine mist which the wind blew back upon him, and on his shirt, and on his freckled arms, and the skullcap which he always wore, because his scalp had been blown away in a mine explosion of which he often spoke.

"Hello, Muriel!" called John Babcock. "Doggone my spots, but you're a pretty picture!"

The front gate jolted and creaked upon its hinges as Jimmy drew it open. "You know how Dad is," he said in apology.

She smiled tenderly upon her lover.

"How's your ma and your pa, Muriel?"

"They're well."

"That's a good thing. You ain't come down for supper, Muriel?"

"I have, if Mrs. Babcock will give me a place."

"Why, honey, she'd eat crackers if she could give you chicken. Hey, Ma! Whatcha think? Here's Muriel come down with Jimmy!"

Neighbors looked out of windows. Muriel blushed.

"I wish he'd stop," Jimmy said, crimson with mortification.

"I don't mind one bit," said the girl resolutely. "It's just his way. I love him, Jimmy."

"Do you?"

"Why, of course. He's your father, isn't he?"

He stared at her like a child. The world of that evening—the distant barking dogs, the crying of Buddie Waller in the next block, the piano banging ragtime in the Murphy house across the street—all were translated into that music of love which fills the interstellar spaces and the heart of God.

Mrs. Babcock thrust open the front screen door. It jangled and hummed as it swung wide. "You don't mean it's Muriel! The darling!" she said.

She was a handsome, fat woman—so fat that it made her head seem unduly small. Now she was wiping her hands on her apron, and now she was tucking up a wisp of hair. The kitchen flush was upon her face.

"Come up here, Muriel. I don't go down these steps if I can help it. I've got a touch of rheumatism in my left knee, lately. I'm getting so heavy, too, you know. Why, it's been years since you came down to us."

"Hasn't it been years?" said Muriel, and ran up the stairs and kissed Mrs. Babcock. "But I remember your sour-milk biscuits."

"Do you, child? Did you hear that, John? She remembers my sour-milk biscuits. Bless her. I'm gonna stir you up a batch right this minute."

"Dear Mrs. Babcock . . . please don't bother."

"It's nothing. I'd love to. Twenty minutes. It'll be that long before the roast is done. I hope you're not tired of roast lamb?"

She drew the girl into the house and turned a beaming smile upon her son. Then the screen door slammed, and the fat form of Mrs. Babcock disappeared down the hall.

Jimmy went to his father. "I'll finish this watering," he said.

"Get away," said the veteran. "I like to do this. You ain't got the patience. I know you. You leave the corners, you doggoned banker!"

"I'm not a banker anymore, so give it to me," said Jimmy.

"Ain't you?" his father said. "Ain't you a banker anymore? A doggoned capitalist . . . maybe that's what you are?"

"I'm fired," Jimmy stated.

"Whoa!" said Mr. Babcock. "Who said that?"

"President Parker said it."

"Get out!"

"I'm not big enough for his idea of the banking business."

"You're not big enough? Hell! Reach me my chewing tobacco out of my right hip pocket, will you? My hands are all wet."

Jimmy sighed and obeyed.

"You ain't big enough!" repeated his father as he stowed the corner of plug tobacco in his cheek. "I'll tell you one thing. You could lick the whole damned set of clerks they got . . . beginnin' with that skinny joke of a vice president. That Callahan gent."

"I might do something in the ring," Jimmy said, changing the subject. "I don't know. I might make good there." And he set his jaw and narrowed his eyes and stared into the darkening evening and the dim future.

"It's the damnedest thing I ever heard of," his father hissed. "Get away from this hose, will you, Jimmy, or I'll turn it on you! I can think better when I'm waterin' or got something to do. This'll take your ma pretty hard, boy."

"Yes," Jimmy agreed, growing suddenly weak. "I'll have to tell her . . . a little later on . . . this evening."

He knew his mother would not talk. She would smooth his hair as though he needed the petting of a hurt child. He dragged in a great breath at the thought of it. Then he noticed his father's keen, practical eyes turned upon him through the dusk of the day, and the water mist from the spraying nozzle.

"Look here, Jimmy."

"Yes, Dad."

"I was just thinkin' of something. You ain't so very old, when you come down to that?"

Jimmy raised a tense fist as high as his head. "Don't say that," he said. "I can stand anything but being made a boy again. I'll tell you how old I am. I'm as old as Adam, by God!"

And he jerked about and stalked into the house.

IV

There was a nursery rhyme, or was it a proverb, which said: "A step at a time will soon make nine."

Jimmy Babcock told himself, as he washed and changed his shirt for supper, that he would take things one by one, and so he would master each detail of his fate—or endure it, at least. There was something about not crossing bridges until he came to them, too. And slow and sure wins the race.

Except on the football field! Or in some of those old stories of guns and gunmen such as his father told him, to weariness. Profoundly he hoped that there would be none of those stories that evening.

He had a chance to whisper with Muriel for one moment before dinner began, and they decided that they would postpone the announcement until the end of the dinner.

Then Muriel went scurrying back to help bring in the soup. There was a great bustle. She was laughing continually, and so was Mrs. Babcock.

They had barely sat down to his father's time-honored formula: "If nobody's gonna say grace, well jus' set and feed, folks!" As Jimmy finished wincing at this remark, the door-bell rang.

"That's probably Dick Lampson with the milk bill," said Mrs. Babcock. "You tell him to send his father around here. I'm gonna tell him what I think of watered milk with chalk in it before I pay that bill."

It was not young Lampson. It was Muriel's father, silent and huge in the semi-dark. He beckoned, and Jimmy Babcock stepped out to him, and followed down to the grass that was still damp.

"I've heard all about it," Aiken said. "The wife's nigh onto crazy. Well, I ain't." He paused. "She's gotta marry somebody. The wife thinks she could fly higher. Well, maybe she could. But if you're clean and go straight, what the hell is the rest to me? I got money enough. I can fix you up, kid!"

"I'll need no help," insisted Jimmy Babcock.

"You'll do what?"

"I need no help. Muriel and I have talked it over. We're going to work it out."

"Say," said Aiken, "don't be in such a sweat to get Muriel's hands into dishwater and baby's laundry. You mean well, I guess . . . but the main thing about you from my angle is that Muriel is fond of you. I guess you're gonna get her, all right. Now, mind you, I ain't gonna horn in. You can run your own cattle. But don't you be a fool. After the marriage, you come to me. We'll talk. No matter how big your head is, you ain't John D. Rockefeller. You can kick a football and hit a tennis ball pretty hard. But that don't make you money."

"I won't have any charity," said Jimmy. "That's all I mean, Mr. Aiken."

"All right. You may wanna work in a laundry, but I got other ideas for Muriel. And I still happen to be her father, no matter how many times she marries. The law can make and break marriages. It can't make and break fathers. You wanna understand that, young fellow!"

Jimmy Babcock said nothing. He felt rather sick, and he stood stiffly silent, wondering how such a flower could have sprung from soil like this.

The big man went on: "I ain't down here to make a fuss. I'm down here to talk sense to you, Jimmy. You'll find me right now the way I'll be ten years from this. I wasn't too good to put my legs under your ma's table and swap lies with your pa in the old days, and I ain't now. I don't change. It's the womenfolk that follow the fashions. But you tell Muriel that if her old woman is mad, her old man ain't. He'd rather hear her bark than anybody else sing. That's about all. I'm going along back home."

He turned toward the gate with a muttered goodnight, but then whirled and came back.

"I guess you know me, Jimmy. You treat her good, and the wallet I carry is yours. You treat her bad, and I'll break your neck!"

Jimmy went back to the house, and when soup was finished, he and Muriel cleared the dishes away in spite of the protests of Mrs. Babcock. But he needed to say a few things to the girl.

"That was your father," he said as they stood in the kitchen. "He's not angry. He wants to put me into business, I take it." He looked at her.

And she, at first expectant, changed under his eye. She said firmly: "I guess we'll fight our own fights, Jimmy."

"We'll fight our own fights," he agreed.

And they went back to the table, Jimmy feeling grim.

It was not an easy meal to him. Two things had to happen. He had to let his mother know of his discharge from the bank, his involuntary confession of failure in life, and after that, there would be the happier news about Muriel.

There was apple pie and coffee at the end, and as he finished his second piece of pie and stirred the sugar into the second cup of coffee, John Babcock broke into the subdued chatter of the women.

"Say, Muriel."

"Yes?"

"You ever hear of the White Streak?"

"I think I have," she said.

"Whatcha hear about him?"

"Why . . . I think I recall hearing he was a great outlaw. Is that right?"

"Sure. What kind of an outlaw, is what I meant to ask? Stick up trains, maybe?"

"He cracked bank safes, didn't he?" Muriel offered.

He nodded at her.

"Your pa has raised you pretty good, Muriel," he said. "You know something. I'll bet he's yarned to you about them days a good deal?"

"Yes. A great deal. He used to tell me stories a lot. About the cattle days, you know."

"Well, it's only ten years back," Babcock reminded her. "It's only ten years back since cows was roped where the Merchant's Bank is standin' right now. The face of the old Dresser Valley has changed a good deal, in that time. Some of the men have changed, to say nothin' of the women." He paused before adding: "They've sure changed their faces, the men have!" He laughed and rubbed his chin.

"Your pa ever tell you about the White Streak and Utah Billie?"

"Utah Billie? I don't think that I ever heard that name."

"He was a bright one, though," Babcock told her. "But he only lasted a short time. You know how the White Streak died?"

"Indians caught him, didn't they?"

"That's what they did. But I'll tell you the inside of it. Utah Billie told me about it. He was a young yegg from Montana way. He knew a safe and a combination four ways from Sunday, and he was as tough as they make 'em. Utah Billie came down into this part of the country and heard about the White Streak, and struck up a partnership with him. They laid their heads together . . ."

"Father," said Mrs. Babcock, "I don't think Muriel is interested in rough stories about bank robbers."

"I am, though," said Muriel. "Dad raised me on them."

"He could," said Babcock. "He used to ride at the head of the posse in those days. He didn't have the same kind of a figure then that he has now, not lacking thirty-five pounds, he didn't. He could sit in the saddle and cut the wind with any man! And more than once he give the White Streak a run for his money. But about Utah Billie. Him and the White Streak aimed to drop down to the reservation and pay a visit to the reservation bank. They framed their job. They got the soup . . . you know what soup is, Muriel?"

"Nitroglycerine . . . I think Father said. Made by cooking dynamite?"

"That's right, I tell you, honey, you been raised right. You got a vocabulary! Well, the White Streak, he furnished the plan, mostly. He furnished the soap, and the soup, and the horses, too. He always knew where to get the best horses. That's how he got his name. When they started after him, he always faded into a white streak of dust."

"Yes," said the girl. And she took the opportunity to smile genially at Jimmy, to prove that she was perfectly happy.

"Now, everything worked pretty good. They got to the bank. They'd framed the night watchman, and he closed the right eye. They got in, run their soap mold . . . Utah Billie was a slick one at that . . . and then they blew the safe and scooped out more than ten thousand dollars. It sure looked sweet to them.

"They dumped the stuff in a sack and got to their horses just as the folks begun to wake up. There was one mistake that they made. They forgot that Injuns wake up and climb onto horses faster than ordinary folks. But the White Streak had the right sort of horseflesh, and him and Utah faded into the moonlight till they could barely hear the mutter of hoofs behind 'em. That plain looked as wide as the sea to 'em, Utah Billie used to say. Just then, Utah's horse put his leg in a hole and broke it, and pitched Utah on his head. The White Streak, he pulled up and stood Billie on his feet. 'So long,' says Billie. 'I'm their meat!'

"But the White Streak wouldn't have it that way. He insisted that they flip a coin to see who'd take the horse away."

"He must have had a fine heart," Muriel said, her eyes sparkling.

"When Utah heard the Injun hoofs coming closer, he changed his mind a little. If there was gonna be a game of chance, he proposed dice. Poker dice was his game. One flop. He handed the box to the Streak, and the Streak threw a pair of fives and a pair of fours. Out there on their hands and knees they studied the faces of them dice in the shine of the moon. It looked hard to beat. But when the young gent took his chance, what you think? Well, he rolled four sixes straight off! The horse was his. He yelled goodbye to the Streak, and off he cut."

"And the White Streak?"

"Them Injuns was a good deal heated up," said Babcock. "And when they caught sight of that robber, they shot him down, and then they scalped him. And that was the end of the White Streak."

"I wished you hadn't told that horrible story," Mrs. Babcock said, shivering. "And there's Jimmy trying to say something."

"I loved the story," Muriel said. "Poor White Streak. He was a brave fellow, wasn't he? What a dreadful end. Utah Billie must have been heartbroken."

"Utah was a hard egg," said Babcock.

V

The four sat at the table quietly for a while. Jimmy had grown red.

"What is it, Jimmy?" his father asked. "Are you gonna make a speech?"

But Mrs. Babcock had a sense of something unusual in the air. "I wish you'd keep still and give the boy a chance," she said. And she looked earnestly from her son to beautiful Muriel Aiken, and then back again.

"I've told Dad," Jimmy began. "But I haven't told you, Mother. I've been discharged from the bank . . ."

"Hold on!" said his father. "You might've waited till I finished my coffee, Jimmy!"

Jimmy's mother reached a hand to the hand of her boy. She pressed her lips to a thin line and stared at him.

"Yes, darlin'," she said.

"Well," said Jimmy, watching his plate with curious eyes, "I saw that everything had crashed. I went to Muriel to tell her that she'd better shake me off, because I'd be no good to anyone."

"Ah, Jimmy," Mrs. Babcock moaned sympathetically. She looked at Muriel, and the girl smiled back. At once, the worry disappeared from the eyes of the older woman. She was already beaming as her boy concluded.

"Muriel didn't see things that way. She says that we can work things out together . . . and so . . . and so . . ." Crimson to the hairline, he lifted his glance to the girl.

"And so we're going to be married!" Muriel cried.

Tears formed in the eyes of Mrs. Babcock, but she did not speak.

Her husband scraped back his chair, then hastily swallowed the last of his coffee. "Why, doggone my hind lights!" he gasped.

Muriel had gone into the arms of Mrs. Babcock. Now she came to the old man, and John Babcock held her by the shoulders at arm's length.

"You understand how it is?" he said. "You live on the Hill, now, and we . . . we run a laundry, honey."

"If only Jimmy is happy," Muriel assured him "What do I care about the rest?"

"You're out of a job, Jim," said his father.

"Yes. I told you that."

"Reach me my pipe off the shelf, will you? Set down, Muriel. I gotta think."

Jimmy brought him the pipe.

"Can't you think without smoking that dreadful old pipe?" asked Mrs. Babcock.

"She's gotta always make a fuss about things," John Babcock confided to the girl. "Don't you get to doin' that, honey."

She smiled at Mrs. Babcock, and the latter smiled back, anxiously.

Blue-brown clouds burst from the lips of John Babcock and strained through his ragged moustaches. He kept brushing these to either side, because they were still damp with coffee.

"Laundry soap won't wash this here clean," said John Babcock. "We gotta think. And doggone my sights, but I got an idea."

"Father!" his wife cried out.

He clouded half the room with rapid puffing. Muriel covertly sneezed.

"Jimmy, you know that I got some land out yonder," John Babcock said.

"Yes," said the young man.

"That land!" Mrs. Babcock shrieked. "Thank God we ain't tryin' to live on it no more."

"Humph," said her husband. "Didn't we live there for eight year runnin'?"

"How'd we live? Like birds in the air!" Mrs. Babcock reminded him.

Her husband answered: "It ain't a bad place, you take it all in all."

"It's too high for the irrigation water to get to it," Mrs. Babcock stated. "And it's too poor to raise grain. All that'll grow there is cows!"

"There's two hundred and forty acres," her husband continued on stubbornly.

"How can you say such a thing? Didn't you sell off eighty acres two years back?"

"Well," said the undaunted laundryman, "that still leaves nigh onto a hundred and sixty."

"And fifty of that is an alkali sink," his wife said.

"Well," cried her husband, "is it a ranch, or ain't it? Will you answer me that?"

"What've you done with it these last years?" she asked.

"Rented it out."

"What you got out of it?"

"I got five hundred dollars, last year."

"Well, and then what?"

"Suppose that a young man was to take a hold of that."

"Yes, suppose that he was?"

"How can you tell? He might make a strike of something."

"What?" the practical-minded wife asked.

"Oil . . . maybe."

"Oil!" sniffed Mrs. Babcock.

"I've seen Parker's own geologist out there, snooping around!"

"He's snooped around the whole county," Mrs. Babcock said.

At this, John Babcock declared: "There ain't any pleasin' of a woman. Look here, Jimmy . . . Muriel! Out there is a ranch. There's a sort of a house on it. It ain't much. There's a few cows, too. Look here. Tomorrow morning, I'm gonna make a deed of that place to Jimmy, if you two want to start life out there."

"What a crazy idea!" Mrs. Babcock said.

Jimmy sat tense in his chair, gripping at the sides of it, gritting his teeth a little.

"We'd be living pretty poor, Muriel," he said.

But Muriel had slipped from her chair and now stood behind John Babcock's chair, her arms around his shoulders and her hands folded beneath his chin.

"But we'd be free, Jimmy," she said.

"Muriel . . . child . . . free of what?" asked Mrs. Babcock, who began to pant in her distress.

"Free of criticism and neighbors and meanness and mocking, and everything!" cried Muriel. "I'd love it. You wait, Mrs. Babcock! I can cook . . . a little. You'd teach me things, wouldn't you? I know something about sewing . . ."

Mrs. Babcock had turned to ice. "Can you milk a cow?" she asked.

"No."

"Can you make butter? Or cottage cheese? Can you put up jellies when fruit is cheap? Do you know how to run a vegetable garden, and keep a berry patch? Can you make bread and cut your own clothes? Can you . . ."

"Hey, let her be, will you?" demanded Mr. Babcock.

"I'm just trying to show her the truth," said his wife. "If you can do all those things, or learn to do 'em, then how about having two or three children to watch? When you go out to milk, one of 'em cryin', one of 'em sick, one of 'em apt to crawl into trouble, and your own laundry to do, and your sewing and patching. And then on Saturday nights, there's a dance . . . somewhere fourteen miles off . . . and you gotta get yourself together and put on your best dress . . . which hasn't fitted for a year . . . and your best slippers with the toes stubbed off of them, and you got to go to the dance with your husband, because he's young, still, and he has to have variety and change . . . well, there's a picture for you, Muriel."

Jimmy managed to say: "Perhaps we could get someone to help, or something . . ."

"On that ranch?" snapped his mother. "Not without finding a gold mine under your doorsteps! Not without luck! Some people have luck. The Babcocks don't! The best that they can hope for is what they'll get out of the sweat of their hands. And half of that throwed away on bad investments . . ." She paused to glare at her husband. "Don't tell me," she said, and sat back in her chair with a great breath, as one who has sent destruction abroad.

John Babcock polished his pipe on the sleeve of his coat, and essayed speech, and failed, and only could say: "Damn! Damn it all!"

"We're young and strong," Muriel said meekly.

"Aye," said the fierce mother. "You're young and strong. You're a beauty, too, my darling girl. Well, I was pretty. I had my share of looks. The young men used to notice me, when I was your age. John Babcock wasn't the only one." She glared at her husband again, accusing him of some invisible crime.

"Look at me!" she cried. "Look at how I've bulged out and spread out of shape! Look at the crook in my back and the bulge in my shoulders! Work, Muriel, work! Look at my hands!" Red and shapeless, she held them forth, a sacrifice.

Pain appeared in the mute face of her husband, but Muriel exclaimed: "Oh, I know what you mean, I think. But I don't think your life has been so bad. See what you've done! You've given the world Jimmy. You've made your husband happy. And that's all I'd want to do . . . to make Jimmy happy, and have a son, just like him . . ."

She choked with fear and joy.

John Babcock took her hands and stroked them, looking at his wife in awe.

And his wife added eloquently: "You've got your youth, and you want to spend it like a drunkard and waste it and throw yourself away. I'd rather see you married to another man, than to my Jimmy . . . and that ranch. Faugh! The smell of the dust is stinging my eyes still, and the hot winds are burning my skin. Look at this cottage. Look around! It's pretty poor. But I'll tell you what . . . it's a paradise to me after what I've been through."

"You see," said Jimmy gravely. "It won't do. I couldn't take you to a life like that."

Muriel said: "I'm going to go, though, if you'll take me. I'll learn to milk, and skim, and churn, and sew, and darn, and patch, and wash, and scrub floors . . ."

"Don't say that!" Jimmy gasped.

He stood up and went to her. Suddenly all three of them were staring at Mrs. Babcock, and she dropped a fat elbow on the edge of the table and covered her face with her hand. Her shoulders twitched a little, and they knew that she was crying silently.

"I'll fix up that deed," John Babcock said in a whisper, "and everything, in the morning, Jimmy."

VI

By noon of the next day, they had finished the details of deeding over the land, and in the heat of the afternoon, the two young people drove out in the delivery Ford of the laundry, which was free for that half day. Jimmy and Muriel sped over five miles of good concrete, through the irrigation district, green as a lawn. Then they reached a bumpy, rutted road, and climbed into the hills. The green disappeared, and brown took its place, and in some parts the naked faces of rock blinked and glimmered like fire under the sun.

They dared not look at one another then, and went slowly on up a steeper and steeper way. The water in the radiator began to boil, and the dust tossed up behind them, gathered in a hanging cloud above them like the plumes of a Greek helmet, and began to shower down. That sifting dust choked them, turned their clothes gray, but at last they came out on the upper level, and twisted from the main road down a narrow alley.

From this, they came out before a little shack in front of which stood two elm trees, scraggly and forlorn, and the sun beat mercilessly down on the roof. That was the ranch house.

They dared not look at one another as they climbed down from the truck and went to examine the place in more detail. It was in sad disrepair. There were three rooms only—the kitchen, where the floor was worn significantly deep between the stove and the sink, and the bedroom, and the living-dining room. Most of the furniture had been removed to the town dwelling. What remained was unspeakably battered and broken.

They climbed to the attic, where a little chamber had been hollowed beneath the roof, and there Jimmy Babcock had lived his earliest years. A broken-legged cot stood there, and, in a corner, they found a toy engine and two cars, rust-eaten.

Then they hurried down the steep flight of stairs to the lower level again, and went out to the rear of the house. The creamery was there, exactly like the house, but still more shaken to pieces. The flooring sagged beneath their steps. Jimmy had a feeling that a chasm lay beneath that floor, deep enough to swallow both their lives. And inside the creamery, where the windows were boarded over, they found the oppressive odor of spoiled milk, sickeningly sweet.

In greater haste they left the creamery and went to the corral down the narrow boardwalk. They thrust the gate open, and the pulley screamed as the rope and the weight drew the gate shut behind them. Then they crossed the dusty corral to the barn. It leaned to the left, and the roof bent inward in the middle. Pigeons whirred out of the loft as they entered, pushing back the sliding door with labor and much noise. They found a few tons of moldy hay in the mow. Everywhere, the daylight glittered through cracks or poured yellow through big holes.

"Well, a hammer and nails and a few boards," Jimmy said at last.

Muriel took a breath. "Of course," she said stoutly.

They left the barn and examined the granary. Rats scampered and squeaked at the opening of the door, and the foul odor of rats was through the place.

"What have they lived on, all of these years?" asked Jimmy in disgust. "Paper?" He pointed to a corner of the room, where a great pile of old magazines had been eaten to shreds. Then they went back to the house.

Now they had seen the worst, and being young and brave, their spirits began to lift with invincible buoyancy. It was very bad, but they could make it better. They could straighten the staggering fences, fatten the wretched cattle, repair that windmill and make it spin . . .

That word brought a rush of pleasant thoughts. With the water from that mill, they would flood the yard, make an alfalfa lawn before the house, create a flower garden, and a vegetable and berry patch, just as Jimmy's mother had suggested.

As for the house, by ripping down some of the old rags of paper from the walls, by thoroughly scrubbing, and by using a little paint, what wonders could be done.

The land? Well, that was hardly a cheerful prospect, and as they stared across the rolling hills, a heavy, hot wind came out of the south and withered their eyes.

Then Jimmy said: "I'll tell you . . . there's no water. The ground's worn out. But work can be fertilizer and water, too. I can work. I can work twenty hours a day! I can make this thing go through."

She looked at him without hope, but with a breaking heart of love and admiration. "Of course we can make it go," she said.

"It's my last chance," Jimmy said. "I couldn't throw it away."

"Of course you couldn't," she said.

"I'll spend a year getting things in shape. Then . . ."

"We'll come out here and do everything together," Muriel declared.

They talked over business details as they went back together to Dresser. They were very serious. The land was clear of any encumbrance, and he suggested that they should put a mortgage on it, and with the mortgage they could buy lumber to repair the house and barn, posts for the decayed fences, barbed wire, a little furniture, paint, and, above all, cattle to stock the barren acres.

She hardly agreed with this. The very word "mortgage" made her pucker her brow; it cast a long shadow of disaster before it! However, those were details which could be settled later. The main thing was that they had made their resolution, and to that resolution they would stick.

* * * * *

He took her in the delivery wagon to her house on the Hill and said goodbye to her for the moment. At the very last, he felt the thrust of pain go through his heart when he held her hand for a moment and felt its slenderness, its softness.

He went away determined to do his best forever, for her sake, but he wished that there was some way in which one could turn blood and agony into dollars. If so, how gladly would he pay!

It was the early evening when he reached his father's house after putting the truck in the garage. His mother sang out to him as he came in through the front door.

"Jimmy, Jimmy! There's a letter here from Mr. Parker!"

He took the thin envelope from her.

"What do you think?" they asked one another in the same moment.

Then he opened the envelope and read:

Dear Jimmy,

It appears that I parted from you too hastily the other day. Will you dine with me at the Club at eight o'clock, tonight?

Sincerely yours,
William Parker

Jimmy took a firm grip on the back of a chair. The nightmare of the ranch slipped off into the past. The bank became his future once more. Like a strong river, his thoughts rushed forward, storming on to a great ocean of success!

All this was in the flash of an instant, and, at his shoulder, his mother had read the words also.

"Great heavens!" she said.

"Maybe it doesn't mean a thing," Jimmy said mechanically.

"No, maybe it doesn't," she agreed. Then she added: "Eight o'clock! You ever hear of people eating that late?"

He did not answer. She had to repeat the question, and then he said he had heard that was the fashionable way.

"William Parker is changing everything around this town," she observed, shaking her head, "even the hours of eating."

Almost in prayer, Jimmy said: "I hope that he'll change my life from what it looked like today."

"Ah, Jimmy! You saw the ranch, of course."

"It looked . . . like a pretty good slice of hell," Jimmy said.

"It is," she said, gripping his arm. "It's hell . . . long, long, hell, with flames . . . and alkali dust. I know."

Hastily he jerked up the letter and read it again.

"He says that he was too quick the other day. What could have made him change his mind?"

"I don't know. Somebody stabbed you in the back, most likely."

"That long, lanky Jenkins . . . damn him," Jimmy hissed. "Maybe. I don't know. I don't accuse anybody. Only . . ."

"Jimmy, Jimmy, it's just like ten years were snatched off my heart and my shoulders now."

"My goodness," Jimmy said, and swallowed hard. "Ten years! Ten millions years." He laughed in a feeble way and fumbled at his mouth and chin, as though they felt strange to him.

"I tell you what . . ." Jimmy began, but he did not tell her, because there was no need.

"It's over," she said.

"No, maybe not. Maybe not. I'm not going to count any chickens before they hatch."

"No, don't do that, boy."

"But if ever I get back into that bank . . ." Jimmy began again. He stretched out both his arms, and bent back his head on his strong, stubborn neck, and flexed his hands. "I'll tell you, Mother, if ever I get back into it, I'll . . . I'll . . . I'll put it in my pocket, I tell you!"

"You'll make yourself so necessary, that Parker can never get on without you."

"You bet I will! I'll show him. I didn't know . . . I . . . I was just like a fool of a kid. You understand, don't you?"

She nodded at him.

"Had I better tell Muriel?"

"Yes, yes. But not till afterward. Not till you're sure. You can't tell what will be said."

"Maybe it's something big," Jimmy said. "If he gets behind a man, he pushes him right to the top. Look at what he did for Aiken. But I won't be a lump like Aiken. I'll work! God help me if I don't work!"

His mother's hand brushed specks from his coat. "What suit will you wear?" she asked.

"Well, what do you think?"

"Why, I don't know what they wear at the Club. But that dark blue suit . . ."

"I guess that's it," Jimmy said. "Blue serge always looks pretty good."

VII

If there was to be a club at all, it should be an exclusive club, William Parker had declared in the first place. At that time there was no one with whom he needed to agree except himself. He bought the ground and built the place, laid out the garden, planted the roses, erected the pergola, and dug out the little lake which, hanging on the edge of the Hill, gave a prospect over the flats of Dresser. Afterward, he gathered to his side ten charter members. They were all rich men, with fortunes based upon the cattle industry, upon the new exploitation of the valley with irrigation, or, last of all, upon the oil wells which were being sunk here and there by Parker and Company.

They knew little about clubs and club affairs. They were all very flattered to be invited as charter members. They were amazed and delighted by the garden, by the spacious rooms, by the soft rugs and glimmering floors. After their first dinner, they sat around the lake and looked over the town, and each thought that he would gladly pay with blood to join this select organization.

They did not exactly pay with blood, but certainly they

paid high. Those ten membership fees reimbursed clever William Parker for all of his expenses and left him holding fifty percent of the stock, the presidency, and the moral kingship of the organization.

When he had established the matter upon this footing, he proceeded to enlarge the Club, but slowly, always selecting men who could be of use to him. What is the strength of an army except its devotion to one tried and talented leader? William Parker could see no use, and therefore he built with care, until he had established himself impregnably. He now ruled the Club with a hand of iron, but he covered the iron so cunningly with velvet that no one suspected this institution, with its good dinners and quiet gambling, was really William Parker's greatest business asset. It was looked upon as a constant drain upon his purse; in reality it was pouring money into his coffers, and when he wanted financial support for a new adventure, he rarely had to go outside of the halls of the Club. Here, it might be said, he had dammed up the resources of Dresser County, and he tapped them forth at his good will. So long as Dresser County boomed, everything went well, and all men thanked him for the wise financial advice he gave them. If Dresser County's boom collapsed, his bank account would not be diminished a penny.

None of these things were known to young Jimmy Babcock. He was only sure that he was walking up to the door of the most exclusive place on the Hill when he approached the Club that evening. He stopped on the driveway and looked at the rosy flush of light in the windows, discreetly shaded from below, and he told himself that this was the realm of William Parker, and here the throne of that mighty man.

When he waited to see the great man, he looked at his fingernails and at his shoes. The window was open. Upon the hot summer wind that voice of Dresser blew faintly in to him, and his heart beat high.

Perhaps, out of this interview, he would gain the ability to climb to such an altitude as this, taking beautiful Muriel Aiken with him. One never could tell. William Parker possessed a magic lamp, which he rubbed for his own benefit and for that of his friends.

Parker came in to meet him, and Jimmy Babcock bit his lip.

For Parker was all in whites, gleaming a little from the laundry iron, and when Jimmy faced him, he wished to heaven that he had not come at all.

However, Parker was a "big" man. That is to say, he dealt with essentials and not with superficials.

Cutting to the heart of his business, Parker said at once: "I wanted you up here, Jimmy, because I wanted to talk to you outside of business. I'll tell you why. As a businessman, you were not exactly what I wanted in the bank. But since you left my office, I've been learning some other things about you. Business is a mask, Jimmy. It covers the faces of men. It turns them into blank eyes that wear numbers. You understand?"

"Yes," answered Jimmy, who did not understand at all. Indeed, he would not have understood his ABCs if they had been placed before his dazzled eyes at that moment.

"I didn't see the mask fall until I discharged you. Now I think that I know the real man in you. I wanted to talk to that real man tonight, as a friend. And then I can explain why I want you back in my business. Let's go in to have a cocktail."

Jimmy had never had a cocktail. He had drunk a little Italian wine. He had drunk prohibition whiskey of dreadful power, and tasted the full horrors of synthetic gin, but he had gone sparingly in these ways of life, for Jimmy had been an ardent athlete most of the days of his youth, and he had never learned what is found in alcohol to take the place of a clear eye, a strong and steady pulse, a hand that does what the brain commands.

But he could no more have refused a cocktail from William Parker than if it had been presented to him by the rosy hand of Bacchus.

"We'll go into the bar," William Parker said, leading the way.

The bar was a small room, dusky and quiet, with the fragrance of many liquors blown about and softly stirred by purring electric fans. There were deep, round-backed leather chairs and little tables with glass slabs over the tops of them, and a smoking stand was at the right of every chair. Three or four other men sat here in the subdued light. They wore whites as well.

And Jimmy writhed, as though he were naked. His stiff white collar clung to his sweating neck and choked him.

"Ah," William Parker announced, "here are some men you ought to know. It will do you good to know these men."

He introduced John W. Beggs, who said: "Say, are you old man Babcock's son? You ask him, does he remember the time him and me hunted down the Little Big Horn, will you?"

He introduced Hiram Littlefield.

"Hello, young man," said Littlefield. "Kinda hot, ain't it? Damn my sights if it don't make me sweat to see you in those heavy clothes. Set down and have a drink, Will, and your young friend with you."

He introduced Oscar Framming.

Said Oscar Framming: "How do you do, Babcock? My boy has told me about you on the football field. How is the laundry business?" And he resumed his paper.

William Parker ordered drinks. An obsequious Negro bowed the frosted glasses onto the table.

"That's what I want," said William Parker. "I want you to meet the representative men of the county. Beggs has enough cattle to crowd the Chicago yards. Littlefield was offered a million and a half the other day for a half interest in his land. Oil, understand? And as for Framming . . . that man's an intellectual giant. He's feeling the pulse of Dresser County. He's liable to inject a couple of million into our blood to quicken the heart rate, too."

He said these things in a low, quick voice. Then he added: "Young men are like young plants. They need good soil, if they're to put out roots. They need good air . . . sun . . . light on their leaves. Well, there you are, Jimmy. Soil, light, water. You can work your way and grow, with people like this on your calling list. You follow that?"

"Certainly," said Jimmy.

He didn't follow it altogether. There was a certain taint of opportunism in this conversation which he did not like very well, but he attributed his sense of the wrongness to his own stupidity, which caused him to lag so far behind the older man.

"Then here's to your business future, Jimmy," William Parker said cheerfully. He raised one glass, and Jimmy raised the other. He nerved himself a little, for he detested the taste of every alcoholic beverage which he had tried up to this time. But the present concoction was very different. It was down before he knew it, with a pleasant and half-aromatic taste of pineapple, as he thought—an agreeable pungency.

"Another dash of a sauce and we'll go in to dinner," said William Parker.

They had another. A curious glow passed over the body of the boy, and over his mind a slight numbness. He had forgotten the unlucky blue serge suit when he went in to the table.

The dining room was as quiet as the bar, but more brightly done. Waiters passed on silent shoes; glassware tinkled musically and faintly, in far off corners. In those corners were all of the diners; the center of the room seemed unused, unnecessary, except that it gave every table its own atmosphere of privacy. And this luxurious waste of space impressed Jimmy immensely.

As they went in to their place, Parker paused at two tables. At each of these he introduced his guest, and Jimmy Babcock bowed to four notables. Then he retired to a corner table which was hemmed in by two great windows. A column rose on the farther side of it; they were pleasantly excluded from the sense of other people in the room.

The mind of Jimmy Babcock was a little blurred. Sometimes, in a pause, he would rouse himself and felt that his host was peering at him with a hawklike intensity. On those occasions, he rather felt that he was an object of prey, and that the banker was about to pounce upon him, but, in his more comfortable moments, he dismissed that impression with a proper scorn.

They had a strong wine for dinner—strong and sweet. William Parker said that it was smuggled in from California. Amazing what fortunes had been made from wine grapes in California, owing to prohibition.

Jimmy nodded. He had heard something of that. But while he listened and tried to make intelligent answers, the fog in his mind increased momently. He was vaguely uneasy, fearing that he would say something wrong. But he knew that he must bear up. He hardly attributed his mental condition to the wine. Wine was a stimulant, he remembered. He drank more of it. Parker saw to it that his glass was always filled.

And, in the meantime, the explanation was to come of why Parker had called him there. What was the revelation that had been made to him that had changed his opinion of the discharged clerk in his bank?

But still the talk was of other things.

What would he have done?

"I was going to be a farmer," Jimmy Babcock told Parker. "My father gave me his little ranch, today."

"And that was where you went with Muriel Aiken?"

Jimmy blinked.

"How did you know about that?" he asked.

The banker looked down. It seemed to Jimmy that, for a moment, the young banker was almost embarrassed. And why? And then other ideas flooded suddenly into the mind of the boy. Why should William Parker have helped Aiken himself to prosperity? What was the impetus? What was the great attraction in the Aiken family, other than Muriel herself?

Ah, but Parker was twice her age, almost. Old enough to be her father, nearly.

And yet not quite. Thirty-five . . . nineteen. Change it a little. Twenty-one to thirty-seven, say. That was not such a great disparity of ages. There were marriages at far greater ones. Jimmy grew more and more confused of mind.

"The vice president saw you off in that direction. He was driving across town. She's a charming girl . . . Muriel is. I think that she was in my mind, when I went to adding up my account of you, Jimmy."

"Yes, sir?" Jimmy said vaguely.

"A fellow who picks the right girl has something to him, eh? Or at least, that's what I should say. And a man who can succeed in one thing has in him the elements of success in everything, my friend."

Jimmy blinked again.

"I hold to a ruthless common sense, Jimmy. Throw aside what I don't need in my business. That's why my business goes. There's no waste material. My organization never is fat. Therefore it runs and doesn't get out of breath. You're an athlete.

You understand that. Now, then, when I threw you aside . . . that was one thing. Then someone in talking to me brought up a little story . . . about a football game . . . high school football game . . . high school had one great star. He was their weight and their strength. The big game comes on. The star is smashed. Two ribs broken!"

Jimmy placed a hand suddenly upon his side and stared. The banker nodded affably.

"His team is getting a licking. Driven back down the field. He has to sit on the bench with his broken side, gasping for breath. Last quarter comes. Then he goes to the coach and says . . . 'Put me in.' 'They'd crush you like an eggshell,' says the coach.

"'Put me in,' says this boy. 'If I go in, they'll watch me. They'll mass on me for the first play. But the quarter will feed the ball to the other halfback. While they smash down at me, the other fellow may get away. He might get loose.'

"The coach was a dog, or he wouldn't have accepted that sacrifice, but he did the thing. He sent in the injured star. The grandstands yelled with excitement . . . then they grew still. And the star was seen dancing back behind the line, making himself seem light and eager. The ball was snapped back. A whirl of players, then, Jimmy. Through the young star's line smashes the enemy. They come like hungry dogs. They leap at the star. They pull him down. They smash into him with knees and shoulders and heads. They want to put him out of that game for good and all.

"And they do it. He lies there limp, unconscious. But down the field goes his teammate, sweeping around a wing of the scrimmage. Hardly watched until he's halfway to the goal line. And that was how the game was won. The star got no applause. He'd done nothing. The coach was ashamed to tell what he had endangered . . . the life of that boy. But he breathed easier when the doctor said that only another pair of ribs had gone. It wasn't fatal.

"You were to live, Jimmy, for you were the boy . . . you were the young star. And when I heard that, my lad, I told myself that I had cast up a false account. I could do without a good many of your qualities. But I couldn't do without that loyalty!"

VIII

So that was the solution.

In addition, Parker was saying: "You know that every man may make mistakes. Of course, I'm like anyone else. I'm ashamed to say so, but it's the truth. I added up the column of Jimmy Babcock, but I left out the most important item. Putting that in, I found you the outstanding man in my bank inside of waste material. I found you a man I could trust. A man I wanted to have intimately connected with me and my life. A man to introduce in my club, to my best friends, a man to start in life with the best foot forward."

He dropped his balled fist lightly upon the table, and Jimmy started from a golden dream.

"My God," said Jimmy, "is it possible?"

"It is," the other said, and his thin lips produced the faintest of smiles. A smile of victory, Jimmy thought at the time, such as a boxer wears when he sees that one of his blows has befogged the brain and weakened the knees of his opponent.

"You're in the clouds a bit, my boy," William Parker observed.

"I was thinking of Muriel. I was thinking that now perhaps I can give her a home worthy of her."

"I drink to Muriel and your home, Jimmy!"

Another glass went down.

"Suppose we go down and try a hand of cards?"

Jimmy went. He was not in the company of a man, but of a god, all of whose decisions must be right. He would follow this great hero, and if loyalty was what William Parker wanted, he would die for him, if need be.

They went down to the game room. Only two tables were taken so far, and on the green felt, little piles of chips were gleaming, red and purple and white and blue. He smiled at them in a happy haze. All the room stirred up and down with his breathing, and the world was filled with lights and kindly human faces.

"I don't know much about cards," he confessed to the other. "I've only taken a hand at poker, once or twice. You see, I never went out much. I was always training. And at the bank, I didn't want to go to work in the morning with a lump of a head on my shoulders. That's the reason."

"Ah," said the other. "Loyalty! I've been blind to you, my boy. We'll shake a few rounds of dice, then, if you want to?"

"Of course. Whatever you want."

"A little friendly game. It eases the end of the day. What stakes do you want, Jimmy?"

"What is played? You'll have to trust me. I haven't much money." He was settled at a table. Of course he would be trusted.

"You'll probably take a pocketful of money away from me," said Parker. "You'll have beginner's luck."

He took from his pocket a dicebox covered brilliantly with

rattlesnake skin, and he produced a set of bone dice, the spots rather obscurely marked with red.

"Indian dice," said William Parker. "Some say that they're marked with blood." And he laughed.

They began to play. Jimmy hardly saw what hands he was shaking for himself. It was poker horses; William Parker kept the record of the winnings and the losses.

"You're a regular plunger," Parker said at last. "Shall we stop there? I hate to keep on when you've lost so much."

But Jimmy laughed. He had lost his bank account. That made no difference.

"You're in the land where gold is dug, not earned day by day," Parker told him.

He played on. There was that ranch that had come into his hands that day. He would play against that. But then his brain cleared a little. He abandoned the drink which kept appearing, refreshed, at his elbow.

"It's a funny thing," Jimmy said, "the way that you're always throwing four sixes."

"It's the way that you talk to them," Parker said, laughing. "They're hearing me tonight. We'll put the ranch in sections. Four parts . . . with a thousand a part. That'll soon put you back on your feet, Jimmy."

"I'd better stop," Jimmy said. "My father . . . Muriel . . ."

"I hate to stop when you're such a loser," the banker said.

"Well, another try, then," Jimmy said. "I tell you what. If luck is with me . . . well . . . the whole thing, one throw, eh?"

"Hello! You want to do that? Blood will tell, Jimmy!"

"What do you mean by that?"

It seemed to him, very vaguely, that his companion drew back just a trifle at this, with blinking eyes. But he could not be sure, and there was every chance that he was entirely wrong.

He threw, and saw three fives and a pair of deuces spin upon the table.

"Full house!" William Parker announced. "Full house. Great Scott, there you are! You have the right kind of luck, Jimmy. And the courage, too! I can see why you've made a go of it in football. A full house to beat."

Jimmy laughed. Huge relief flooded through his mind. He was safe; safe from himself, from his father, and Muriel would never have to know about this.

Released from tension, his brain relaxed suddenly and grew dim, and the lights in the room and upon the polished edges of the table quivered and leaped again.

"You'd better take your try," he said. "It's not really fair, though. I shouldn't have said one flop. We've been playing horses, all along."

"It's hard," admitted the banker. "But fair for you is fair for me. I won't welch, Jimmy. I hate the puppy who goes back on his game almost as much as I hate the yellow dog who doesn't pay his gambling debts."

Jimmy shuddered.

"Yes," he said, and he swallowed with difficulty. "Go ahead, sir. "Maybe you'll . . . maybe you'll rap out another of those four six-hands."

"I?" the banker said. "I?" Then he shrugged his shoulders.

"The luck won't follow me like that," he said. "I never can do anything at poker. They'll tell you that at the Club. Poker cards or dice, all the same. I have no luck."

He rattled the box close to his ear. John Beggs came up close to the table.

"That's a funny box, Will," he said.

"Funny-looking. Indian stuff. I thought I'd change my luck, if I could. Sammy May trimmed me for a couple of thousand, the other day." He lifted the dice up close to his face. "Talk to Uncle William. Come out and shine for me, little bright eyes. Here you are . . . thank . . . you . . . kindly."

"What is it?" asked Jimmy Babcock, suddenly trembling.

"There's luck, for you," Beggs said. "Four sixes on the first throw!"

IX

When he wakened the next morning, Jimmy Babcock was in a state of fluttering uncertainty. His heart beat irregularly. His head was full of wavering impulses, and a bell rang faintly in his ears. He wakened from a dream into a dream. Everything was unreal, and when he came out to breakfast, he found that it was very late. His father was already gone to the laundry, and his mother had kept hot coffee for him, and she brought eggs and bacon hissing hot from the kitchen.

He stared at the food dimly, with no ability to eat, and only gradually he forced himself to swallow a few morsels. His mother sat opposite him, talking of nothing, smiling contently and with a deeply expectant eye. He knew what that expectancy meant. She wanted to know the result of his interview with the great banker the evening before, and he had no answer to give her.

What if he were to tell her that William Parker had made him a confidant, had expressed a desire to make him a partner in his affairs, and had talked to him with the intimacy of an old friend?

Yet the truth remained that the same man, in the same evening, had stripped him of his bank account and the ranch!

However, there would be a sufficient explanation of that, he had no doubt. He knew, now, that he had drunk too much, and doubling the tips of his fingers into his palms, he swore to himself that he never would be such a fool again. That vow he registered dimly in his heart, for keeping.

But if Parker had taken so much from him when he was under the influence of alcohol, the older man certainly would not keep his advantage.

Jimmy allowed himself to say mysteriously to his mother: "I have to go to see Mr. Parker at the bank this morning. When I come back, I can talk to you, Mother."

Then he finished his coffee with a gulp and went back to his room. There he took the deed to the ranch, stuffed it into a coat pocket, and set out for the bank.

He grew more at ease when the hot sun beat on his face and his breast, because it became more and more obvious that Parker was not a cad and not a cur. Therefore, he could not rob a drink-befuddled young man in his club and keep the proceeds. Perhaps he intended this as a lesson.

However, a little shame-faced but thoroughly confident, Jimmy Babcock entered the bank and nodded carelessly at a few curious faces that stared at him from behind the bars of the cage. They thought that he was down. They would be surprised to find how up he was, before long, when the strong hand of the bank president began to push him forward again.

He was admitted at once to the president's private office, and there he found William Parker looking as fresh as ever, and cool on this hot morning. He shook hands with Babcock with a smile and asked how he did.

"A little groggy," Jimmy confessed, with a purpose in his

mind. "I'm not used to liquor, and last evening is a good deal of a blank in my mind, except that I know I lost the ranch. Here's the deed to it. I have to sign, I think . . . there are some witnesses needed, I believe, and a notary . . ."

"Oh, we'll fix that up," Parker said airily. And he winked at Jimmy Babcock.

However, strangely enough, he went on with the matter of the deed. And in a trice the thing was done. Jimmy had sat at the presidential desk and taken the pen from the presidential hand, and duly signed away the ranch. The notary was gone. A boy had taken the deed off to be placed in Mr. Parker's private safe.

The speed with which this was accomplished made Jimmy a little dizzy at first, but then his head cleared, and he looked at the president with what was, frankly, a very hungry eye.

Something was to come to him. What?

"And now, Jimmy," said the president," I have a very busy day ahead of me."

Jimmy arose, obediently, but at the door he gathered courage. "I don't want to bother you, sir," he said, "but last evening you spoke about taking me back into the bank . . ." He paused. It was not modesty that stopped him, but a sudden terror, for he saw in the eyes of the president a light keener than the light in the eyes of a hawk, and he saw a cruel, small smile upon Parker's lips. He dared not interpret that expression, and there was no need.

For Parker almost immediately explained himself by saying: "Jimmy, you're young. You're so very young that it hurts me to let you see the facts. I invited you to the Club, last night. I wanted to test you. Very well. I gave you a swinging start. I wanted to see what you would do when you were given your chance to meet the best people in the county. You didn't meet the test, my boy. You lost your head, made an ass of yourself, began to gamble, and threw away your patrimony, to put it shortly.

"Let me ask you if, in justice to my depositors, I could employ you in any responsible position about this bank. No, Jimmy. Not even as a porter, or a doorman."

Jimmy clutched the knob of the door. The words boomed in his dizzy ears.

And then he heard Parker's voice going on smoothly: "I can give you what may turn out to be a better thing for you than a position in the bank. You're a young man, and you need experience in the world. You need a chance to settle down and learn how to be a man. You weren't a man last night. You were a boy, and nine parts fool. Go to Canada and work in a lumber camp. Go to Australia and sail there before the mast. That will make a man of you. I'll tell you something more. You've made a horrible mess of things here, and your life in Dresser is bound to be a failure because you've crashed at the beginning. Dresser is too small a town for a man to recuperate after such a blow as your fortunes have received. In a larger city, you might dodge about a corner and start again, but here, everyone knows you, and everyone knows what you're worth. Take a new start, Jimmy, and in addition, take a check from me. I'll give you five hundred dollars. You can pay it back when you're on your feet. That'll simply be an affair of your own honor. You understand? It will buy you a ticket out."

Jimmy came slowly back from the door, breathing hard, as though he had been stopped in a plunge at the line, and were returning to his position resolved to smash through on the next play, and at the same spot.

He said carefully: "Mr. Parker, it's plain that I was a fool last night."

"I'm glad you see that," said the president of the bank. "Now, as I said before, it's a busy day with me, Jimmy."

"I know that you're always busy," Jimmy said. "I wonder

how often you've been busy before, feeding liquor to fools and then trimming them?"

William Parker rose. "That'll be all from you, Jimmy," he said. "Pass on through that door."

Jimmy smiled. In a scrimmage that grin of his had flashed and taken the heart out of the opposition. "You're old enough to be president of a bank," he said, "but you're young enough to hit."

And he started a beautiful long left for Parker's chin. It never arrived at its mark. The hand of William Parker flirted in beneath the flap of his coat and came out again, garnished with a little bulldog revolver, short, stubby, and with an appallingly wide mouth.

Jimmy recovered himself violently, almost lost balance, and toppled into the gun, and then drew back.

"There are all sorts of ways of playing a game and scoring a touchdown," said William Parker pleasantly. "You have ten seconds to get through that door, my boy."

Jimmy ground his teeth. "I'll have your hide for this, Parker," he said.

"You have five seconds left," said the president, "and after that, I'll shoot you down like a dog, my lad!"

There was not the slightest doubt in Jimmy's mind that Parker meant what he said. There was a smile still, to be sure, but there was an unearthly cruelty in it, and a slight flare to William Parker's nostrils.

Jimmy turned and went through the door, and beyond down the corridor and into the street.

He walked on in a trance. The world had changed. His own mind was so speeded up that all other movement seemed reduced to a ridiculous gait and became like a slow-moving picture. He could see the horse that trotted by with a delivery wagon pick up every hoof in turn. And a sparrow fluttering over the edge of a building seemed to be hanging almost motionless in the air, going on in little pulses, and then halting, dead still. The people who passed him were not walking. They were lifting their feet and putting them down again on the same spot. A smile was a frozen picture of a grimace, gradually enlarging. And in Jimmy's own heart, there was born a vast and a fierce desire.

It was unlike any emotion that ever had come to him before. Only once, on the football field, had something faintly like it overwhelmed him. He had gone down in a heap of tacklers, and as the pile disentangled itself above him, he had seen a foot drawn back and deliberately driven into his face. On that occasion he had caught the ankle of the man and drawn himself erect. It was a big, wide-shouldered center, sneering at him.

"I'm going to get you," Jimmy had said.

And he had gone madly at the man on the next play—madly, but with his eyes open, his brain as cold and as clear as pure ice. So, dipping down, he had applied his shoulder and the drive of all his weight behind it, to the knee of the heavy center, and heard and felt the crunch of breaking bones—heard it with icy chills of satisfaction.

And the same coldness was in his brain at this moment, the same clearness of eye and of thought, the same deliberation, swift as the flash of a bird's wings.

He had to get at William Parker and crush him, as he had crushed the big center. He wanted to feel Parker in his hands, and smash him, and feel him turn limp. He smiled as he thought of this, and that smile was a new expression upon the face of Jimmy.

X

He found himself, suddenly, at the farther end of the town, the familiar square face of the high school before him. He passed the wall of the bleachers and heard the familiar, angry, barking voice of Riley, the football coach.

It was morning, and, of course, Riley was getting in some early fall practice. So Jimmy Babcock went inside and stood with a hand dropped upon one hip. The full team of last year's victories was lined up against a ragged array of scrubs. There were pink-faced boys with frightened faces, trying to be brave, desperately struggling under the lash of Riley's tongue. He was a good coach, was Riley, but a devil incarnate. He was young; in another year or two, he would be working with a university team.

He saw Jimmy.

"Hey, Jimmy boy. I'm glad to see you. Step into a pair of shoes and trousers, will you, and help those scrubs give my boys a workout? Or are you too fat for that, Jimmy?"

Jimmy went gladly to the dressing rooms, changed into sweaty football togs, worked his toes against the rough, cleat-set sole, and walked out onto the field. It would give him a chance to burn up some of this dreadful superfluous energy that was shooting in his nerves and in his veins like so much electricity. Riley had gathered the scrubs about him.

"You kids, now you're gonna have a chance. You know Jimmy Babcock. You've all heard about him. He's going to work out with you. Watch him, will you? He has stuff, unless he's forgotten what I taught him."

He dragged Jimmy aside and said fiercely in his ear: "Watch yourself! Look at those young tigers I got over there. They're varsity stuff. They average a hundred and seventy-five. They're men! Look at 'em."

They were men indeed, lean, bronzed, and trained by the labors of the hayfield, the mine, the lumber camp. They were capable of a man's labor. To them, this game, even under a broiling sun, was still a joke. When Jimmy stepped into his place behind the line of the scrubs, he saw those regulars looking at him with no awe in their young faces. They would have regarded a grizzly bear without fear, and Jimmy was pale.

He laughed, and said to his young quarterback: "Feed me the ball, my boy. What's your best go?"

"Around end . . . or a forward pass. We can't go near their line. They tear us to pieces!"

"I'll try their line," said Jimmy. "I need exercise."

He stood calmly, lazily, and watched the snap of the ball. Instantly the regulars were through the scrubs, and half a dozen fierce faces were bearing down upon him. But they seemed slow to the coldly burning brain of Jimmy. There was a little gap between the wide-swinging tackle on the left and the straight-driving guard.

The ball floated toward him like a puff of gauze. He gathered it from the air with one hand and started, swerved through two pairs of reaching hands which he barely felt, and then darted through that gap. A halfback with a contorted face lunged at him. He met that solid bulk of mountaineer, labor-hardened, with a straight arm that floated the man away. Then he ran on, slowly, easily, wondering at the speed with which the white bars jerked away beneath his feet. The quarterback, last line of defense, was dancing before him, arms outspread. Jimmy doubled over and charged straight ahead. There was a shock. He was down; gripping arms slid easily away from him as he rolled to his feet and jogged on to the goal line, grounded the ball, and turned.

The players, far behind, were already pulling up in their sprint to overtake him. The quarterback was a motionless heap on the grass. Riley came up. His voice whined sharp and thin like the bark of a bull terrier. He was cursing his regulars. He was telling them that they were wooden images, not football players. He would bench them all for the season and play the scrubs.

"Now line up again! Do that once more if you can," said Riley, and picked up his winded quarterback by the back of the jacket.

Jimmy laughed softly, for his heart had been just slightly eased.

"I'll do it again," he said to the regulars. "I'm coming through the same place, boys."

"You'll be damned first," said the tackle and guard in one voice, and they crouched in their places, their teeth bared, and their eyes narrowed.

Once more they brushed through the defense at the snap of the ball. Once more the ball seemed to stick in the air like a bubble in water. It was a low throw, to the right, but spearing it with one hand, Jimmy Babcock saw from the corner of his eye that the charge of the regulars was straight and true—no gap among them.

Then he caught his breath, turned himself into steel, and

hurled forward straight at them. He flung himself low, low as the knees, flying shadowlike over the ground. So he crunched home into a yielding mass. He heard groans and curses. Big hands gripped him, and the fingerholds sprang away from his writhing body. A huge arm caught around his throat, but he plucked that arm away like a bent straw. His cleats found the turf, and with a wrench he was through. He split the difference between two converging backs, spun round and round with the shock, but could not go down. It was as though the only weight was in his feet and the rest of him was air. Then down the field again. Again the dancing quarterback, this time with a white, desperate face.

Pity came faintly into the heart of Jimmy Babcock, and he merely dodged catlike to the side and went on to the goal. He turned back to see faces of despair. The scrubs alone rejoiced, and Riley, for once, was silent.

At last he came to Jimmy and said sourly: "What you been doing to yourself?" He poked a finger into Babcock's chest. "You're India rubber," said Riley. "I won't break up my team on you. But can you forward pass still?"

"I can do anything," Jimmy said, and laughed again, for subtly he was soothed and pleased by this cheerful game.

The regulars limped back into position. Some of them were shaking their heads and walking unsteadily. Others were wiping clots of turf from their faces. They looked at him without fierceness now. They were like children before a parent.

Jimmy said to his left end and halfback: "Tin-can down that field when the ball snaps. Go forty yards and then turn around. I'll drop the ball in your hands. Mind you, you won't be able to drop it."

And so it was.

He waited for the ball and then for the charging line.

Lightly he avoided the first tacklers, danced back half a dozen yards, and then threw. High and fair as a punt, that throw looped through the air. He had no doubt of its termination, but, dodging the tacklers again, he saw the yellow-brown bubble float softly down, and settle in the arms of a bewildered scrub. Then he walked off the field.

Riley forgot his team and went with him, tore his clothes off, stared at his naked body.

"You look soft," Riley said hoarsely, "but you're not. Jimmy . . . kid . . . you could melt through the hardest line in this country like you were a knife and they cheese. Why didn't you go in to college? Look here! It's not too late. You could go now. It's not too late! Twenty-one. You're just ripe for it. It's not too late."

"It is too late," Jimmy Babcock insisted.

"Why, kid? Why?"

Jimmy laughed again. "I've other things to do," he said, and stepped beneath the shower.

"I dunno," Riley said, chin on fist. "You don't look so much. You look soft . . . but you ain't! You're India rubber. My God, I never saw . . ." He stopped, and snapped a hopeless pair of fingers in the air.

"If I had you," Riley said fiercely. "Anywhere! If I had you, I'd smear the Blue, I'd smear the Red. The little old championship of the United States is all that I'd collect with you in my pocket, baby! Get the hell out of here. You've ripped the heart out of my team and given me the blues for the season. Get the hell out of here!" And with wrinkling eyes of fondness, he stared at the boy.

And Jimmy went back to the town with a step that was lighter than ever, and with a heart that was still soothed and that beat like a happy promise in his breast.

Something had happened to him, and he did not know what it could be, but whereas the world and life in the world had seemed a strange an insoluble problem before, now everything was quite simple and quite easy.

William Parker, for instance.

It had been years ago, surely, that he had thought William Parker was a great man, a man to be followed, a man who held the future in the hollow of his palm. Now it was very different. He could see that the banker was a thin sham. He, Jimmy Babcock, would one day poke a finger through that glistening sham that looked like hard, bright steel, and show the town of Dresser and the rest of mankind that William Parker was a sneak and a crook and a cheap scoundrel.

After he had shown the world that, he would take Parker in his hands and break him in two.

They would not hang him. Yonder lay the quivering horizon, over the hills, where the law could be dodged, or else broken through like a football line.

He laughed again, to himself, and then turned toward the laundry, because of course he must do the honorable thing at once, and break the news of the great loss of the ranch to his father. He would simply tell that news, and he would make no promises. But, afterward, he would remake the money that he had lost. He would make it fairly, or unfairly. By theft and craft it had been taken from him, a boy. But now he was a man. That was the difference between the dull fellow of yesterday and this new creature, like a shock of electricity, prepared to jar the world and split open certain doors of entry.

Laughing he reached the laundry, and laughing he entered his father's office.

XI

John Babcock sat in his shirt sleeves, on account of the warmth of the morning. Those sleeves were rolled over his hairy forearms to the elbow and showed a purple patch of tattooing of a dog guarding a hat and with the large caption: EVER FAITHFUL!

He had seen that motto many times before, but now it appeared to him truly absurd for the first time, for he could remember what the hypocrite, Parker, had said about loyalty—and to think of that was merely to laugh forever.

John Babcock sat cocked back in his chair, with his heels upon the edge of his desk. He turned his head and arched a liquid volume that glinted in the air and fell neatly into the mouth of the spittoon.

"Peel off your coat, Jimmy. You look pretty fit. But you must be hot."

"Never was so cool in my life," said Jimmy.

"Well, you look cool, too. You look fit for poker, Jimmy. That's what Utah Billie used to say. You got to be cold, Utah used to say, before you can get the hot money. You got to keep cold, Utah used to say, before you'll get the stuff that'll warm you. Utah was a hard case, Jimmy. You remember me talking about Utah and the White Streak before?"

"About five hundred times," Jimmy said. "I've dropped in to have a chat with you, Dad, about . . ."

"Five hundred times?" said John Babcock. "Well . . . maybe I have, and maybe Utah was worth repeating on five hundred times, and what do you think of that, me boy?"

"I don't doubt you," said Jimmy, and yawned a little. "What I wanted to tell you is worth repeating, too, five hundred times five hundred, I'll have you know."

"Did I ever tell you about the time Utah stuck up the Oregon stage?"

"You have," said Jimmy dryly. Then, seeing that it would be difficult to turn his father from the thread of his thoughts, he said: "Whatever became of Utah Billie? I've never heard anyone but you talk about him."

"Of course you ain't, because he was only a flash and then he disappeared. I was about his only partner."

"You and the White Streak," Jimmy said, yawning again.

"The White Streak . . . sure. But he didn't last long with old Utah. What become of Billie? You ask a mountain what becomes of the pebbles that are washed down its sides. There'd be more sense in that, me boy. Look what the West is?"

"Sure," said Jimmy. "I've seen a little of it."

"And what does it look like to you, kid?"

"It looks like a lot of sunburned grass, and cows with their ribs sticking out, and the sun burning up the rocks. That's what it looks like to me, if you want to know."

John Babcock looked upon his boy through a silent moment. "You've stubbed your toe on something," he said. "Was it William Parker?"

This was Jimmy's opening, but he was unable to take advantage of it in talk as he had been able to take advantage of openings on the football field that morning. His father's talk was an invincible flow that defied interruption for more than an instant.

"But out here in the West, when you've lived longer," said John Babcock, "you'll begin to see that your eye fools you, the same as Utah Billie's hand could fool your eye."

"Sleight of hand, eh?" said Jimmy. "I don't think you ever told me about that before."

"Didn't I? There's a lot I haven't told you, Jimmy. But about the way things change. Out here in the West . . . it's like smoke. The wind blows it away, and the wind blows it back. Mountains and everything! I've seen mountains that nobody could climb when I was a kid. Hardly hadn't names, in those days. Now, lady schoolteachers, they eat picnic lunches on the top of 'em! Those mountains have growed small."

Jimmy saw that this was rather an allegory, and he smiled and nodded. There was a certain vein of speech in his father that he could appreciate richly.

"I've seen deserts that a lizard couldn't live in without gettin' heartburn," went on the elder Babcock. "Right there where the lizard scratched its ear and wondered which way to go, they now cut five ton of hay per acre per year. I've seen a state that was a month across . . . and now it's twelve hours from side to side. You understand?"

"Partly," said Jimmy.

"So do I," said his father, "and anybody that thinks he understands it all is a fool."

"Parker understands it all," Jimmy said.

"All of a bank," answered his father quickly, "which a bank ain't as mysterious as one cow bawlin' for its calf, when you come right down to that. He might understand the mind of a bank, but a bank is made up of dollars. And one screechin', roarin' mustang would take more pages of definin' in Webster than the whole damned bankin' system of the whole damned world. And I'm right about that!"

"I think you are," said Jimmy. "I haven't felt a horse between my legs for a couple of years," he added thoughtfully.

"I've seen horses that you couldn't put between your legs," said this invincibly rambling conversationalist. "I've seen 'em that when you thought you had 'em tight, you clamped your knees down on a whiff of white cloud up in the sky. That's what I've seen. But that's changed, too. The whole West, it changes like water flowin'."

"Why has that changed?" asked the boy. "Horses will still buck."

"Not like the old days. They've bred 'em tall and sleek, and all legs and neck. I've seen horses that could turn around between your legs. I've seen horses that could turn and catch hold of their own tails, like snakes. Them horses could pitch, and don't you make no mistake. I've seen horses that could pitch you off and tie you in a figure eight while you was sailin' toward the sky. They used to have horseflesh in these parts. They got legs now." He drawled it in a high disgust.

"And so," he concluded, "I can't tell you what become of Utah Billie. He was in the current, and he must've flowed far. Because he was the kind that would float."

"Unless he was salted down with lead, eh?" said the boy.

"Him that tried to salt down Utah Billie, he got seasoned good and proper before his gun was out of the leather. To see Utah snake a Colt out from under his coat was worthwhile, lemme tell you! And he tagged you with a bullet while you were winkin' your eye at the sun."

"I've heard a lot about these hard men," Jimmy said with scorn. And he shrugged his shoulders.

"You have, have you? And you take it with a grain of salt, maybe?"

"I do," said Jimmy Babcock. "I think if it came to a pinch, I might make some of those hard men eat their guns."

"What's made you proud this morning?" asked his father.

Jimmy snapped his fingers in the air. "You have some extra guns here," he said. "I'm going to start wearing one. Let me see that drawer."

He pulled it open. There were no fewer than five long Colts reposing there. From these he selected one, uninvited, spun the cylinder, saw that it was loaded, and bestowed it in his clothes.

"That's my favorite poison, kid," his father said coldly.

"Well," said Jimmy, with equal coldness, "you're not using poison these days, I take it?"

"Are you?" asked John Babcock. "The last I seen of your target practice, you weren't first rate, kid."

"You haven't seen me practice today," answered the boy. "My hand is steadier. I've learned the trick." And he laughed soft and low, as he had laughed before on the football field. He had no doubt of himself. Nerve and muscle and brain, all were at peace with one another. Nerve and muscle and brain had been worked together into a new metal, and tempered as tough as leather and as hard as steel.

John Babcock looked gravely upon his son. "What's been walking on you, son?" said he.

"William Parker."

"You don't say. William Parker? I thought you put him in your pocket the other day?"

"He took himself out, and that wasn't all he took out of my pocket."

"How come?"

"He took my savings, and the ranch, too."

The elder Babcock whistled. "Well, well," he said, "that's quick work. That's what I'd call a man-sized shuffle. How did he work it?"

"With a dicebox made of rattlesnake skin," the boy said carelessly.

Not an ounce of emotion appeared in his face or in his voice. He could have laughed at bleeding hearts at that moment.

"A dicebox made of rattlesnake skin?" said the other, shaking his head. "You mean that you shook dice with him?"

"I did. He took everything I have, at his club."

"With dice, eh?"

"And alcohol," Jimmy added. "He seemed to think he needed old King Alcohol to prepare the way for him, for this easy killing."

"He took everything?"

"He did."

"And what did he give you in exchange? Even a trade rat leaves an exchange."

"He gave me some advice."

"Like what?"

"To get out of the country," Jimmy said calmly. "Australia, he said . . . or a Canadian lumber camp, would be about my size."

"Well, well, well," murmured John Babcock. "Who'd have thought of that."

"I didn't, for one," said Jimmy.

"I bet you didn't."

"But I may take his advice."

"About leavin'?"

"Yes. Except that I may have a little job on my hands before I go."

"About leavin', Jimmy . . ."

"Yes?"

"You might duck that, for a while. We could talk it over on the way home to lunch."

"I'm eating out," Jimmy said, and left the laundry.

XII

It was in Jimmy's mind to go straight to the Aiken house and say goodbye to Muriel, but he hesitated. Although all of his ways were straightforward, he knew that there was a time when diplomacy was better than brute force. And it would be a tearing, painful scene. Perhaps a letter would do as well, would make the break equally final and formal. The coldness of a letter, too, might raise her pride, settle her sooner in her determination to think no more of a homeless runagate.

From the corner, as he came to this decision, he looked back at the laundry, and saw the steam rising from the chimney, and the puffs of black smoke, and heard the whir of the machinery. It was an ugly little building, but it had paid better than cattle. A gun is an ugly thing, too, but it might pay better than banking, from his viewpoint.

He sauntered on.

Far away to the south, the east, the west, the hills rose softly, overlapping their lines, one upon the other, as easily journeyed through as the flat, for a strong automobile. But the nearest hills were to the northwest, and these were not automobile country.

There was nothing to see but the dead bones of the earth's structure there, ugly heaps and piles of rocks, broken strata whose shattered ribs protruded. Now and again a cactus stood up in unashamed ugliness, and then there were a few of those hardiest trees like willows and lodgepole pines which found rooting, here and there, in crevices of the earth. Above these ragged hills, the dustier mountains arose, less barren, more grand. They had forest too inaccessible to tempt the lumber man, as yet. Among those forests there were little valleys, pleasant spaces where small farmers, here and there, had built houses. Old-timers still trapped and hunted those woods. A thin stream of pelts came down after the winter snows had cleared the way.

To the far blue of those mountains, young Jimmy Babcock turned a determined eye, and in the smaller half of a second, he made up his mind. It seemed to him providential that his conversation with his father had turned upon the subject of horses. A good tough horse, in that direction, would laugh at the pursuit of the fastest of automobiles. And an automobile-mounted party could foam in vain about the lower hills; it would have to continue on foot if it wanted to overtake him there.

When he had made up his mind, he took out his wallet and counted his cash. He had a little over two hundred dollars. It represented the sum total of all the wealth that he had saved at the end of twenty-one years of life.

"However," Jimmy said to himself, "I'll make it grow, after a while. It's gotta grow into a horse first."

He knew the place to go.

The Wycherley hay, grain, and coal yards kept, as well, a filled corral, stocked with horses for the cattle range, and from those corrals the cowpunchers bought their mounts when they left town at the beginning of the season. To the Wycherley yards he went and passed through the driveway, where the gravel was stained black by coal dust, to the inner heart of the domain, where the horses were kept in several corrals. He found his mount at once—a tough-looking roan mare, with a ragged mane flaring above her ears and a scraggly tail that looked as though it had been combed thin by cactus spines. He tried her under the saddle and smiled as she pitched and struggled to get out the kinks of high spirits. When she came to herself, she was quick on the rein, intelligent, light-footed. Last, he put her at a low rail, and she jumped it in good fashion. She would be the thing for cross-country work.

So he paid a hundred and sixty dollars for her, and got a ragged old secondhand bridle and saddle for another forty. They would hold the mare for a day.

After that, he went on to other purchases. In a dry-goods store, he bought some black cloth—"for lining a coat." At the gun shop he bought some dynamite—"to blast out some stumps near the house." Incidentally, he picked up fifty rounds of ammunition for a .45-caliber Colt.

Then he left the town and went down into the "jungle" which stretched up and down the creek on either side of the railroad bridge. This was the calling place of wandering tramps and yeggs and all that floating population that goes by train and never buys tickets. He would be secure from town observation here, since the police never went down to that dangerous ground unless they had to, and even the most curious and daring of the youngsters feared the "jungle" with a consuming horror.

In this thicket he came upon a pair of oldsters boiling up their clothes in a battered washboiler. They looked at him with bleary eyes and sour faces, but he did not stay for words. He went on until he found an empty corner, and there he started his work of rendering down the dynamite and securing the nitroglycerine which was its strength.

He knew all about this process of cooking the "soup," because his father's tales of the White Streak and the exploits of that famous yegg had familiarized him with the necessary details. Also, while he was in the "jungle," he fashioned the black lining he had bought into head gear which would cover his entire head. He placed and cut the eyeholes, allowing for them liberally, and gave the skirt of the mask enough length so that it could be pinned down under the collar of his coat. For he could remember well the story of how the White Streak had the flap of his mask blown across his face, and how the whole crew of the stage jumped him in that moment.

All the craft, the daring, and the skill of the Streak hardly had rescued him from that danger. He, Jimmy Babcock, would not allow the thing to happen to him.

Dusk had thickened the trees of the "jungle" before he was finished, and as he walked across the town toward his father's home, he could see the lights shining from the houses on the Hill. They were like bright stars, and somewhere among them was Muriel Aiken. So he turned his back resolutely with a distinct and chilly feeling of having said farewell.

It was a silent supper table at which he sat that night. His father grumbled, once or twice, at the slowness with which bills were paid to the laundry. His mother complained that the apple and quince jelly had not jelled; for the rest, she watched the cold, set face of her son and said not a word. Apprehension was in her eyes, and he clearly saw it there.

He went to bed early, heard his father's rocking chair creak for a time on the front porch, and then fell asleep. He did not need an alarm clock, but knew, accurately, that he would waken between one and two. It was a quarter past one, in fact, when he sat up in bed with a clear mind and a body tingling with expectation. Then he dressed.

He took a pair of whipcord trousers, old riding boots, two flannel shirts, a canvas hunting coat, a battered felt hat, and when he was dressed, he looked at himself in the mirror and smiled at the somewhat pale image. The mountain sun would cure that fault.

He had bought his main necessities; the other things he now collected one by one from the house, and from the work-shop behind it where his father spent Sundays at a foot-powered turning lathe. At last, he laid out his kit on his own table. He had the "soup" in a small flask, a length of fuse, a quantity of the soft yellow soap that was used in the laundry, his gun and ammunition, his black mask, several pins to hold down its flaps, matches, and a short, powerful steel bar from the shop. The White Streak was never without a "jimmy" and this would serve for that purpose. He was completing this survey when he thought he heard a hushing sound in the hall, such as may be made by the brush of a stockinged foot. He listened a moment. The wind sighed faintly through the window, and he made up his mind that his imagination had been working. Then he gathered up his belongings, stowed them comfortably, and opened his door.

The hall was black, empty, and he went slowly down it in his stockinged feet, carrying his boots, and taking care to step close to the wall, as the White Streak did, on such occasions. The reason was that his weight on the floor exerted less lever-age when his footfall was near the nails that fastened down the boards.

At the door of the room of his parents, he paused an instant and thought of them not as they now were, asleep, but in the morning, when his mother would knock and call him to breakfast and receive no answer but silence.

The front screen occupied him for some moments. Its hinges were full of squeaks, but as the White Streak had so often, there is no door in the world which can't be opened in silence. A soft and steady pressure, long maintained, did the work, and eventually he was on the path in front of the house, where he pulled on his boots and crossed the lawn.

He leaped the picket fence and glanced back. It seemed to him that a shadow passed across one of the front windows, but this was readily explained, for a half moon was hanging in the sky, and the clouds that blew softly across its face trailed shadows such as that which had crossed the windowpane.

So Jimmy Babcock went on across the town to the Wycherley yards, and there he demanded the roan mare of the night clerk.

"What for at this time of night?" the clerk asked, for people on night duty never are polite.

"I'm jogging down to the marshes with a couple of friends," said Jimmy. "We might get something."

"Sure you will. You'll get malaria," said the clerk, and led the way to the corral.

The roan was soon saddled, and stepped out of the Wycherley yard in the most noonday spirit of alertness. Nothing could have been more cheerful than her manner of going, with her head turned a little to the right, as though she were studying the face of her new master with one eye and the face of the road with the other.

He tethered her in the lee of the poplars in the empty lot that adjoined the bank, assembled all his necessaries, weighed his Colt in his hand, and then stood for a moment to survey the bank.

XIII

It was just after two o'clock. The moon was nearing the zenith, and through a gap in the clouds he saw for an instant a big red star. Jimmy Babcock appropriated that star to himself. It was his star of destiny, and red in sympathy with his wrath. As for the bank itself, it looked an impregnable Gibraltar. The recessed windows showed the thickness of the wall, and the low, squat structure seemed designed to resist shocks of all sort.

"The face of a bank is like the face of a man," William Parker was fond of saying. "You read its character there."

Dresser County agreed with him, and never a depositor went past the Merchant's Bank without a nod of reassurance. However, Jimmy freshened his grip upon the steel bar, and his confidence did not wane.

Around the rear corner of the bank came the night watchman with a quick step, paused, and looked straight at the poplars which shaded young Babcock. He went on again to the front of the bank, paused again, looked to either side, and then disappeared on his round.

At his demeanor, Jimmy Babcock felt much concern. He

knew the man—a burly ex–prize fighter with broken metacar-
pal bones in a ridge on the back of each hand.

"I got one punch in each mitt," he used to say. "And after
that I got a slingshot. And after that, I got a gun."

"The gun comes first, when you're guarding this bank,"
Parker had directed him.

He was a stupid fellow, however, and on that stupidity
Babcock had counted heavily. Now Pete Cross seemed galva-
nized to a new life—stealthy as a big cat, he stole about the
bank, making many pauses, like a hunter on the trail.

Jimmy went to the rear of the jail and crouched behind
a pile of newly arrived boxes until the watchman went by a
second time, again wavered at the corner, and then passed
on. He was no sooner started than Jimmy, fumbling at his
mask to tug it more snugly into place, started for the back
door and inserted the edge of the bar beneath it. In the
first upward surge, it gave without a squeak. At the second,
the bar of the lock snapped with a soft sound that proved
it was poor steel, and the door puffed gently open with a
breath of air from the inside of the building. In that breath,
Jimmy Babcock distinguished that smell of paper, bound
ledgers, and the thin, disagreeable odor of ink which he
always associated with the inside of the bank. To others of
the clerks, as he knew, the place was an inspiration. They
felt their hands upon the vital pulse of life. But to Jimmy
the bank usually brought a sense of writer's cramp and an
ache between his shoulders.

He actually stepped back a trifle from the door, and as he
did, out of the corner of his eye, he saw the wide shoulders and
the brutal face of Pete Cross, and the gleam of a gun rising in
the watchman's hand. He simply had reversed the direction of
his rounds and had caught the robber red-handed!

The White Streak used to say: "The hand is faster than the gun!"

The hand of Jimmy, as he spun on his heel, flicked cleanly home upon the chin of Pete Cross; the prize fighter dropped his weapon and went backward drunkenly, his knees giving beneath him. The second blow was a cruelty, but it could not be avoided. It dropped Pete Cross in the light of the moon, and there he lay without quivering, while Jimmy Babcock lashed his arms, his ankles, his knees.

"Never forget the knees," the White Streak had always said.

Pete's own pair of handkerchiefs were used to gag him.

"Listen for his breathing, if you can hear it, he ain't gonna choke," the White Streak would say.

Then Jimmy took the man by the heels and dragged him inside the door and laid him face down at one side of it.

"If you kick around and make a noise," whispered Jimmy," I'll rub you out."

"Nobody can recognize a whisper," the White Streak always said.

And now Jimmy stood on the field of his labors and felt no great alarm. It was only twenty minutes after two, as he assured himself. The watchman was disposed of beyond criticism. The door of the bank had been opened with ridiculous ease; the door of the cage did not need to be opened so long as he could climb.

And climb Jimmy did, like a monkey. He unscrewed a couple of the sharp spikes that topped off the fence and swung down on the inside.

The major difficulty was the making of the mold from the soap, and in this he exerted the greatest care. For the White Streak always had impressed upon Utah Billie that it was better to spend an extra hour in danger constructing an accurate mold than it was to fire the shot and leave the door shattered but unopened.

So around the almost invisible crack of the door, he worked the mold by degrees. It was a round door, the most difficult kind, and it was fitted in with a wonderful closeness. Rubbing one's fingers across the surface, it was difficult to find the crack.

He was not awkward, and he knew almost exactly how the thing should be done; it was as though the ghost of the White Streak stood at his shoulder and directed him. However, it was his first job. It was half past three, as he assured himself by a rapid consultation of his watch, when something scraped on the wooden floor of the bank.

He turned as a cat turns, with his gun ready. There was no doubt about what he had heard. He had switched off the well-shaded electric light as he whirled, and now he strained his eyes into the dark, unable to see a thing, but perfectly certain that another human being was yonder in the obscurity.

Pete Cross, perhaps, having loosed his bonds? He thought not. He felt an odd assurance that even if Pete did sever his bonds, he would run for help rather than tackle the robber of the bank single-handed.

Then a voice said close to the fence: "Hello, Jimmy. Are you in there, son?"

All the skin of Jimmy's body contracted in prickles, and sweat came hotly out. It was his father!

John Babcock said: "Wait a minute, Jimmy. I'll have a light, here, in a minute."

A ray of light pierced the dark and fell, with wonderful suddenness, straight upon Jimmy's face.

"Open the door," said John. "Don't look at me like a tiger. I'm not going to call the police, boy."

Jimmy went to the door. "You'd better go home," he told his father.

"I'd better not," said his father. "Have you run the mold yet?"

"Yes. That is . . . I want you to go back, Dad."

"Whatcha know about pouring in the soup?" asked his father. "You'll put in enough to knock the roof off the bank . . . or else you won't put in enough to faze the door at all. Open up a way for me, Jimmy, will you?"

"I can't manage this lock, I'm afraid," Jimmy said, realizing with sudden relief and guilt commingled that his father had actually appeared as his confederate in this work. "Wait. I'll try the pry again." He tried it.

Alas, for the locks of William Parker's banks. It gave with a loud snap. The door fell open. The elder Babcock entered.

He carried a hooded lantern in his hand.

"You guessed that I'd do this!" exclaimed Jimmy at once.

"You wouldn't sit down and let Parker walk up and down on you, I guess," said the father. "You had to hit back at him, and what other way was there for you to punch? I figured it out, sort of."

"You saw me leave the house?"

"Sure. And while you were asleep, I found your flask."

"Of nitroglycerine?"

"Of soup. Yes," corrected the laundry owner. "Lemme look at this mold." He flashed a ray of light upon it and nodded almost at once.

"You got the right idea, Jimmy. Wait a minute. Look at the corner you've put on here. I've seen the Streak run a mold with his own hands and a match for a shape." He chuckled a little. "But the Streak had practice, Jimmy. This ain't so bad. Now gimme the flask."

Jimmy held the lantern, putting a bright spark upon the

little soap funnel which topped the mold, while his father poured in a thin trickle with a heavy hand.

"This ain't the best soup in the world," John Babcock said in his bright and cheerful way, making this adventure most matter-of-fact. "This ain't the best, but it's good enough. If it can get its shoulders under the edge of that door, it'll lift it off, I reckon. There . . . That'll do. Where's the fuse?"

Jimmy could do no more than play lantern boy from that moment. His father took complete charge of all of the preparations, always acting without haste, and once or twice nodding and chuckling to himself.

"I wish the Streak could see me now, Jimmy," he said. "I wish that Utah Billie could, too. Why, all comes so natural to me, as if I'd done it fifty times before."

The work was finished, the fuse laid and lighted, after they had packed layer after layer of rugs over the face of the door to deaden the sound of the explosion. Then they retreated to the farther corner and lay flat upon their faces, their hands over their ears.

"Will it go?" murmured John Babcock.

That instant, the spark disappeared under the rugs, and the next there was the strangest sound that Jimmy Babcock ever had dreamed of. Even the words of the Streak could not adequately describe it, for there was a distinct shock, and yet the thing was softly done. He felt the breath compressed in his lungs, and his head whirled, and yet it had been less like a cannon than like the cough of some indescribable monster.

"We missed," John Babcock said, scrambling to his feet. "And now let's get out of here. We missed, Jimmy, though I felt sure that we'd lift that door off."

Jimmy backed against the rods of the cage wall and set his teeth, as though he had been cornered here by a visible danger.

"We can't have missed," he said at last. "This has gotta go through!"

He unshuttered the lantern and poured a long ray straight at the safe. They had not failed. The door was not blown off its hinges, to be sure, but better than that, the lock had been burst, and upon its hinges the door had swung wide. The checkered brightness of the steel drawers gleamed like water from the interior.

XIV

The section of the drawers which were used by William Parker occupied the lower left hand corner, as Jimmy Babcock well knew, and in a moment the steel bar was at work on them. Their locks yielded readily. The first one contained a mass of newspaper clippings, and some of them were growing mellow with age. Clippings which dealt with the rise of William Parker from his first appearance in the town of Dresser. The second drawer was drawn out with a jerk that flung rattling onto the floor a dice-box bound in rattlesnake skin, and a quantity of dice.

"Hello," Jimmy said. "The very ones that he used with me. Look at that!"

"We'll just take 'em along, then," John Babcock said, and carefully picked up the dice, one by one.

Jimmy Babcock fell into a nervous frenzy. He explained in a stammering voice that the dicebox could be recognized by anyone in the county. That certainly all the members of the Club had seen it, and that it would be the readiest means in the world of fastening guilt upon them.

John Babcock simply brushed this argument away with

a laugh. "I like the look of these Injun things," he said. "And maybe they'll bring us luck, in spite of what you think."

There was certainly no time to argue. From the same box that contained the dice, they picked out a fold of legal paper, which proved to be the deed, and then and there old John Babcock touched a match to the document and watched it burst into sudden flame.

"That brings the land back to me," he said. "Go on, Jimmy. Get the next box open."

"I've got what I want," Jimmy said. "I've taken back what he took away from me. And now I'm ready to go. What was that?"

"The wind. That's all. You've taken back part of what was taken from you, but all the same you got more comin' to you. Look how it is . . . you've spent a lot of misery gettin' up to this point. He's gotta pay you for that. You maybe have formed a bad habit that'll stick to you . . . and he's gotta pay you for that. You've lost sleep, you've dragged your old pa out of bed, and you've sure run a chance of spending fifteen years in jail. Well, he's gotta pay for all of those risks and those chances, too!"

"I'm through," said Jimmy. "Dad, come along. I wouldn't touch stolen money."

"Stolen rot!" said his father, and, snatching the jimmy from his son's hand, he instantly pried open the last four boxes of William Parker's section of the safe.

When he had done that, he rapidly pocketed the contents, which consisted of labeled envelopes. His pockets bulged with it, and Jimmy Babcock stood by and ground his teeth in an impotent rage. Nothing but physical force could make his father leave the place until he had gutted those boxes.

"Now, for God's sake . . ." urged Jimmy at last.

"It's not four yet. We got time. Look here!"

He blew open the end of one of the envelopes, the last of

which he was putting into his pocket, and Jimmy saw a sheaf of banknotes, compacted solidly.

At last John Babcock would move, and yet he was far from willing. He groaned, as he looked over the bright faces of the rest of the steel safes.

"This here is a trick that the Streak never would have missed," he said.

"Damn the Streak!" Jimmy Babcock burst out. "I wish I'd never heard his name. I wish I hadn't! It's the story of him that has brought us both, probably, to the door of a jail. The devil take him."

They left the cage through the broken door. They went rapidly down the passageway to the rear door.

"Don't blame the Streak," said John Babcock, speaking with astonishing disregard for the volume of noise which he made. "If you'd been the Streak, William Parker never would've got this much bulge of you. The Streak showed you how to get even with him."

"Where's Pete Cross?" Jimmy muttered, beside the back door.

Then, with an exclamation, he darted outside. Even by moonlight it was possible to see where Pete Cross had dragged himself across the gravel and rolled onto the grass beyond. He explained rapidly to his father, but John Babcock, as ever, refused to be disturbed.

"He's gone for help . . . well, but he's too late," said John Babcock. "Let's go home."

"Home? I'll never see home!" the boy said bitterly. "I'll start for the hills, pronto."

His father took his arm. "Don't you be a fool," he said. "What about Muriel . . . if you was to lead that kind of a life?"

"Muriel will stay behind."

"You'll never see her, either, I suppose?"

"I'll never see her, Father."

"You young fool," said John with increasing warmth. "You gonna ride away?"

"I have to, Dad."

"You got a horse, here?"

"Yes, beside those poplars."

"Get on that horse, and ride straight home, and take this stuff with you. I'll come along and meet you at the shack behind the house. There's enough of the cow's hay to make a feed for your horse. Hurry!"

"Dad, you don't seem to understand. Every suspicion will point straight at me."

"Why will it?"

"I can't stand here talking. They'll be back at any minute. You don't seem to realize that Pete Cross is raising them. But as for suspicion . . . well, who else would have stolen the deed? Who else would it be any good to?"

"Go get on that horse, and ride it home," said the father. "Leave this here town, and of course you're the robber, and you're outlawed, pronto, and every dirty job that's happened here inside of the last ten years is sure to be dropped onto your shoulders. But stand up and face it out, and put your shoulders against the wall. You hear me? Get onto that horse, and ride him home to the shack behind the house."

The weight of age and the authority of experience were upon the side of John Babcock. Besides, he was so seldom positive that this certainty of his had enormous weight.

Half sulkily, as though he were sure that he was doing the wrong thing, and yet glad to let another bear the responsibility for his actions, Jimmy went to the horse among the poplars, mounted the pony, and rode away.

The alarm burst out behind him before he had gone a block,

and as he turned down an alley's mouth, he heard a gun begin to fire rapidly, as fast as the ejector could flip out used shells.

Pete Cross, a little late, had certainly been able to bring help, and Jimmy shuddered a little when he thought his father had brought them both to capture by his policy of delay.

Jimmy rode straight out of the town toward the marshes, then doubled about, and cut in to the town of Dresser in such a way that he was soon behind the family house. There he dismounted and led the mare to the cowshed, unsaddled, fed her, rubbed the dust from her fetlocks. There must be no proof of the direction in which he had gone with the mare, and he had heard of animals being traced by the mere color of nature of the dust and mud on their hoofs.

He felt quite satisfied with his cleverness in thinking of this minor detail. Then he went out into the naked moonlight and found his father sitting on a broken apple box and whistling at the sky.

"You'd better get to bed," Jimmy said hastily. "Great God . . . suppose they were to find you up at this hour and . . ."

"Have you still got that pretty black mask?" asked his father.

"I'm going to burn it," Jimmy said.

"No, give it to me. I'm going to bury the envelopes, wrapped in it. I've had a look at the inside linings of these here, Jimmy. What would you think is in them?"

"I don't know," said Jimmy. "Whatever it is, I don't want any part of it."

"Sure you don't," said John Babcock. "I ain't offering any of it to you, for that matter. You got the deed and the dicebox. I've got the dice and the money . . . and there you are. But I just thought that maybe you'd have a touch of curiosity to know?"

"Well?" his son said impatiently.

"There's more than eighty thousand dollars in negotiable bonds and such stuff. And there's more than fifty thousand dollars in cash sealed up here."

"A hundred and thirty thousand!" cried young Jimmy.

"It makes you feel a lot better, don't it?" John Babcock affirmed. "It's right next to a first-class shooting scrape . . . a haul like this here. Where'll I bury it, Jimmy?"

"Wherever you please," young Babcock said gloomily. "I'm going to bed. Here's the mask, if you want it. But, Dad, God knows that I give you my advice out of my heart. I wouldn't touch Parker's money, if I were you."

"Wouldn't you?" said the laundryman. "Well, you ain't me, and there you are. And we both got our wishes, as you might say."

Jimmy shrugged his shoulders and smiled a little at the whimsicality of this. Then he went straight on to the house, pulled off his boots, and entered the place with the greatest care. He made no more sound than a cat as he stole down the hall, and he was in bed, staring with great eyes up into the vault of dark above him, when he heard his father down the hall. He could not sleep. He lay wondering what peculiar intuition had stirred in John Babcock that night to make him so excessively wakeful—he whose snoring was so famous and so prolonged on ordinary nights. Still pondering this odd problem, Jimmy fell asleep. He slept soundly, sweetly, without a dream.

When he wakened in the morning, there was a rapid hand beating at his door, and the voice of his mother exclaiming: "Jimmy, Jimmy! Get up! Get up! There's been a robbery. The bank's robbed, and there's no end of trouble. The whole town's wild. Come out and hear about it!"

"Who's here?" asked Jimmy.

"Nobody but Marshal Fuller," she said.

Marshall Fuller! On only one occasion had the grim marshal troubled him, and that was when he had caught him up a neighbor's peach tree and switched him thoroughly.

XV

He stepped into his clothes and looked anxiously out the window, at the same time wondering if it would not be better, even now, to make a break for the horse shed, mount the roan, and flee. But that idea had no sooner come into his mind than he dismissed it again.

There was no purpose in a flight of that sort when a half-dozen high-powered cars would instantly be sent in pursuit, to cut him down long, long before he could get to the rough region of the hills. He finished his dressing, therefore, and walked out to the front porch, where the marshal was sitting with Mrs. Babcock.

"Marshal Fuller wants to talk to you," she explained. "You've been working at the bank so long . . . he thinks that you may have some suspicion of one of the employees. Shall I leave you two alone, Marshal?"

"Thanks," he said, "maybe you'd better."

She hurried into the house, only pausing at the door to explain, with frightened eyes: "They've carried away tons of money, Jimmy! Whoever heard of such a thing!" Then she went in.

Jimmy looked at the marshal and found that it was easier for him when he was meeting the rather bleary eye of the officer of the law.

Marshal Fuller said: "I wanted to talk to you, Jimmy. The way that your ma says. We've chatted with all the boys in the bank except you."

"Was it an inside job?" asked Jimmy with innocence.

"Sure it was. The crooks knew which were Parker's boxes, and they went through them all. They didn't touch anything else."

"Yeah. That looks pretty inside," Jimmy admitted thoughtfully. "How'd they get in?"

"Soaked the night watchman and knocked him cold."

"Slingshot?"

"Nope. Fist."

"Wasn't Cross on duty?"

"Yes."

"I thought he used to be a prize fighter."

"I guess he's kind of brittle in the jaw. Anyways, from the lump on the side of it, you'd think that a mule kicked him."

Jimmy put his left hand in his pocket. He was conscious of a small bruised place, the size of a dollar, on the back of it.

"What did they do afterward?"

"Only one showed up at first. He was the one that put Cross out, and then tied him and gagged him and dragged him inside of the door. He went on to do his work. Then after a while, Cross saw another man come in. Looked older. After a while, Pete found that he could move by rolling and hunching along, and he got out of the bank and headed for the first house. He had to go slow. The work made him nearly choke on the gag, and he was half strangled, but he managed to start an alarm by picking at a door. By the time anybody could come, the job was finished. The two were gone."

"It'll be a bad thing for the bank," Jimmy said seriously.

"Pretty bad. Pretty bad for the yeggs, too, if we can catch them. Yes, Judge Wender will give them plenty, because he's a great friend of Parker."

"He is. That's true."

"Have you got any information about 'em?"

"Not much. I hoped you might have an idea."

"Not any."

"None of the other boys at the bank seemed to be down on their luck, lately."

Jimmy considered. "No," he said, "I can't say that they were."

"Parker particularly wanted me to come to you," said the marshal. "He said he'd come along himself, after a while. He seemed mighty anxious to have me talk to you. Seemed like he suspected that you might know something."

"Did he?"

Suddenly the marshal leaned forward. "If we could get one of the two to confess, I think that we'd take state's evidence. That and the money, you understand?"

"I suppose you would," said Jimmy.

The marshal spat over the edge of the porch. "Jimmy," he said, "I hate to say this, but it looks like you're the one with a motive."

"What kind of a motive?"

"There was a deed . . ."

"Oh, you mean that," said Jimmy airily. "The one that I lost to Parker, you mean?"

"I mean just that. The deed was missing along with the other stuff."

"Of course it was," Jimmy said, and he pleased himself by being able to laugh. "Of course it was gone. I'll tell you what happened. I lost the deed to Parker at his club. I'd had a little too much to drink, and after dinner we shook dice. I lost everything! I thought, the next day, that Parker was going to keep what he won. He even called in witnesses when I signed the deed over to him. But after they left, he told me that he was just giving me a lesson, and he gave it back to me."

"Hello!"

"That's right."

The marshal studied the lie. It was not a very strong one. "Parker don't tell it that way."

"Don't he?"

"No, he don't. Not a bit! He says that he put that deed in his safe . . . meaning to give it back to you afterward, but wanting the lesson to soak in for a while."

"Humph!" said Jimmy. "He couldn't be double-crossing me, could he?"

"Where is the deed, Jimmy?"

"I burned it, of course. There it was with my signature witnessed, handing things over to Parker. Of course I burned it. That passes the land back to my father."

The marshal looked earnestly at him. "I want to believe you, Jimmy," he said in a quiet voice as he glanced around the yard. "Here's Parker himself, and your father."

They came up in Parker's big, shining automobile and climbed down to the ground. Parker came up the path first, and gave a look and a nod to Jimmy.

"I'm going to talk to you inside, Jimmy," he said. "Babcock, I want you, too. Marshall Fuller, can you amuse yourself out here on the porch, for a while?"

"Certainly, Mr. Parker."

They passed into the parlor. It was closed with a smell of varnish and faded flowers. Jimmy jerked a window open.

"I want to talk to you both," said Parker. "I want to talk to

Jimmy, and I want you to listen to the evidence. You may help to bring him around to reason, John."

"Why, Mr. Parker," said the laundry owner," you seem sort of all heated up, don't you?"

"It's enough to heat up any man," said Parker. "I'll tell you in one word. Your son has joined himself to some experienced thug, and they've looted my bank."

"Hey? Hold on!" said John Babcock. "What you say to that, Jimmy?"

Jimmy smiled. "It's rot, of course," he said.

"Is it?" answered Parker. "I'll make you take that rot pretty seriously, before long."

"Blaze away, then," said Jimmy.

William Parker sat back in his chair and, for a moment, stroked his narrowly pointed beard, which gave him the look of a man of another century. That beard had been worth many thousands of dollars in giving Parker's bearing some weight.

"Do you know that your boy gambled away his deed on the ranch to me?"

"I know about that."

"That was his impulse to rob the bank, Babcock! I was keeping the deed for a few days, simply to give him a lesson before returning it."

Jimmy smiled sourly again. "You were keeping the two thousand in hard cash, too, were you?" he said.

The lips of the banker twitched. "Babcock," he said, "I've drawn a wall around your boy, and he can't get away from me."

"Well, well, well," said John Babcock. "I'm a reasonable man, Mr. Parker, and I'd like to hear what the wall is."

"Jim," said Parker, "yesterday, you bought some dynamite."

"Well?"

"What for?"

"None of your damned business," Jimmy said pleasantly.

Parker's teeth clicked together.

"Answer him, Jimmy," said John Babcock.

"To . . . to blast out stumps . . . in the lot, there," said Jimmy.

"Where is that dynamite, now?"

"We sent it out to the ranch."

Parker smiled grimly. "The ranch, eh? You see how quickly your lies run to the ground? In what did you send it?"

Jimmy was silent. There grew in him a conviction that he would soon have to kill this man. He reasoned it out calmly, without passion. He would give the talented Mr. Parker an equal chance to get out his gun.

Parker did not press that point, but began nodding impressively at John Babcock.

"Yesterday you bought some ammunition, a length of fuse, and a horse, among other things. Why the horse?"

"To ride, if you want to know."

"To ride to the poplars beside the bank, in the middle of the night. And there to stand. Why, Jimmy? And why was it just at the time of the robbery? You can't dodge that, we traced the horse by a crooked shoe on the left forehoof. We traced it from Wycherley's to the bank, and from the poplars toward the marshes, and from there straight back to your house. It was an easy trail. My detectives showed it to me." He nodded. "It didn't take long to put men on your trail, Jimmy, as soon as I knew about this work. And I'll tell you what I'll do. I'll jail you for twenty years, unless you let me know who the second thug was and where the money was put!"

XVI

As he made this proposal, he leaned far back in his chair again and smiled at Jimmy Babcock with eyes that twinkled like stars on a frosty night. And Jimmy stared back at him with a growing sense of impotence, and a growing hatred.

"I've tried to deal well with this boy of yours, sir," Parker said to the elder Babcock. "I've tried to help him out of town. I've offered him a five hundred dollar ticket away from Dresser. He wouldn't take it."

"Well, well, Jimmy," John Babcock said, shaking his head.

Jimmy said not a word.

"We have a case against your boy now," Parker declared, "that will convince any jury. Blind men could see that he's guilty. He's taken a hundred and fifty thousand dollars' worth of stuff from my safe. I want that money back, and I want the name of the experienced yegg who helped him. Because the lad's too much of a fool to have done such a slick piece of work. Otherwise, I tell the jury that he lost money to me, and a deed. That he signed the deed over to me, that I discharged him as a drunken spendthrift from my bank, that he refused my offer to leave Dresser and accept a substantial check for his start in a new part of the world . . ."

"Leaving Muriel Aiken to you?" Jimmy suggested.

Parker half rose from his chair. His color changed, and bright anger flared in his eyes. Then he settled back again, his mustaches twitching.

"The boy's mad," he said.

"Never seen the least token of it before today," said John Babcock cheerfully.

"We'll go on with the case against him," the banker said, keeping his eyes fixed upon the boy with a sort of hungry malevolence. "Having established a perfect motive, then I show that he bought a horse for flight, but changed his mind and decided to stay at home and brazen the thing out . . . that he bought dynamite for the purpose of preparing 'soup' . . . that he bought fuse, also, and that with his horse he left Wycherley's yard in the middle of the night and rode straight to the vacant lot beside the bank, at just about the time that Pete Cross was attacked. Now, Babcock, what do you think a jury would say to that?"

"Why," said John Babcock, "I'd say that it looks tolerable black for my boy. But then, you can't tell how things would turn out at the last. There's always the last chance, you know."

"Is there?" Parker said, lifting his brows with sardonic politeness.

"Ever tell you the story of the White Streak and Utah Billie?" the elder Babcock asked cheerfully.

"Babcock," the banker said, "don't you think you could find a better time for your yarns than this?"

"Why, it won't take a minute . . . and it shows about how things will turn out," said Jimmy's father. "Shows you what a last chance is like. You ever hear of the White Streak?"

"A yegg, I think?" the banker replied restlessly.

"Yes, him and Utah Billie, that was a bright young gent, cleaned up the bank on an Indian reservation, and they lit out with the Injuns swarming after 'em. Billie's horse put his foot in a hole and busted a leg, and the Streak offered to shake dice with Billie for the one horse that was left. Billie was fond of his hide, it appears . . . and he took the chance. The Streak throwed the dice and got a couple of pair. Then . . ."

"Who told this story to you?" Parker asked in a strangely cold and even voice.

"The Streak told it to me," said John Babcock.

"I thought that the Streak was killed and scalped?" Jimmy said, irritated by this inopportune storytelling.

"He was shot down and scalped and left for dead," John Babcock confirmed, "but bullets don't always kill, and more than one man has lived after his hair was lifted. Set still, Utah, you skunk."

Now the amazed eyes of Jimmy saw that a long blue Colt had slipped into the hand of his father and was aimed steadily at the banker. And, with his left hand, John Babcock lifted the skull cap which he always wore and showed the horribly blotched and corrugated skin of his head.

William Parker passed the tip of his tongue across his lips. He said nothing at all.

Babcock, settling the skull cap back on his head, took from his pocket the dice box made of rattlesnake skin. He placed it gently upon the table.

"The White Streak decided to go straight, after his hair was gone. He shaved off his beard and his whiskers. He got a ranch. Afterward, he went to work in a laundry, and finally owned the business. Utah Billie done just the opposite. He let his hair grow on his face, fixed himself up with a brand new name . . . and banking was his long shot."

Parker shuddered so violently that his eyes closed; the skin of his cheekbones and cheeks was puckered gooseflesh.

"No jury in the world would believe you," he said, gritting his teeth.

"Wouldn't they?" said John Babcock, alias the White Streak. "Wouldn't they believe it if I told 'em where to go to look up pictures and fingerprints, and all?"

"The rope that hung me would hang you," said Parker desperately.

"I never done no murder," Babcock said. "Neither would I have to talk up your past. All I'd have to do is show the folks of this here town a rattlesnake dicebox, small size, with two sets of dice, and one of 'em loaded to roll four sixes every flop."

Utah Billie, at last, shifted his eyes toward the door. Footfalls sounded hastily on the path, on the porch. And suddenly John Babcock put away his gun, and only just in time, for Muriel Aiken stood in the doorway.

"Uncle John!" she cried, seeing only him, at the first. "What have I been hearing . . . that some dreadful suspicion was . . . Jimmy, what does it mean? It isn't true!"

John Babcock said: "You mean about the robbery?"

"Yes, yes!"

"Why, honey," said the elder Babcock, "would it be likely that if there was a suspicion hanging onto Jimmy, William Parker would be here havin' a friendly little game of dice with us?"

Her pale face relaxed.

"I knew it wasn't true," she said in a trembling voice. "Only . . . only . . ."

"Matter of fact," John said, "Mr. Parker has just been in here makin' a wonderful offer to Jimmy. He wants him to take a ten thousand a year salary and a big slice of the stock."

"Ah, Jimmy," Muriel responded, trembling with joy.

"Mr. Parker," explained the laundry owner, "has been workin' too hard, and he sees that he's gotta take an extended trip, and so he wanted to leave the business in the hands of a good, steady, responsible man. Jimmy is pretty lucky, at his age, I'd say."

"William!" cried the girl. "You say it . . . to make me know it's true."

Parker affected old and courtly manners. Now he took the hand of Muriel and kissed it.

"I couldn't resist Jimmy's wonderful talents at the game of dice," he said.

THE MASKED RIDER

I

If Señor Francisco Torreño had been a poor man, the bride of his son would have been put on a swift horse and carried the fifty miles to the ranch in a single day, a day of a little fatigue, perhaps, but of much merriment, much lighthearted joyousness. However, Señor Torreño was not poor. The beasts which he slaughtered every year for their hides and their tallow would have fed whole cities. Sometimes he sold those hides to English ships which had rounded the Horn and sailed far and far north up the western coast of the Americas. But he preferred to sell to the Spaniards. They did not come so often. They offered lower prices. But Torreño was a patriot. Moreover, he was above counting his pence, or even his pesos. He counted his cattle by the square league. He counted his sheep by the flocks.

To such a man, it would have been impossible, it would have been ludicrous, to mount the betrothed of his only son and gallop her heedlessly over the hills and through the valleys to the great house. Instead, there were preparations to be made.

The same ambassador who negotiated the marriage with the noble and rich d'Arquista family in Toledo had instructions.

If the affair terminated favorably, to post to Paris out of Spain with all the speed of which horseflesh was capable, and, from the same coach builder who supplied the equipages of Madame Pompadour, to order a splendid carriage. About the carriage Señor Torreño mentioned every detail, except the price.

Chiefly he insisted that the exterior of the wagon should be gilded with plenty of gold leaf and that in particular the arms of the Torreño family—that is to say, an armored knight with sword in hand, stamping upon a dying dragon—should appear on either side of the vehicle.

All of this was done. The sailing of the Señorita Lucia d'Arquista was postponed until the carriage was completed and had been shipped on a fleet-winged merchantman for the New World. And, when the lady herself arrived, she was ensconced in that enormous vehicle as in a portable house. For it was hardly less in size!

Twelve chosen horses from the estate of Torreño drew that carriage. They had been selected because they were all of a color and a size—that is to say, they were all glossy black without a single white hair to mar their coats, and their shining black hides set off the silver-mounted harness with which they were decked. In the front seat, lofty as the lookout on a ship, was the driver, a functionary of importance, shouting his orders to the six postilions who, with difficulty, managed the dancing horses, for these were more accustomed to bearing saddles than pulling at collars.

In the van of the carriage rode a compact body of six men from the household of Torreño, mounted upon cream-colored steeds. Six more formed the immediate bodyguard around the coach itself. And, finally, there was a train in the rear. These were composed, last of all, of ten fierce warriors, well trained in Indian conflicts, skillful to follow trails or to take scalps, experts with musket and pistol and knife. In front of this rear guard, but still at a considerable distance from the coach, jour-neyed the domestics who were needed. For, at every halt, and on account of the wretched condition of the road, the carriage was sure to get into difficulties every three or four miles, and a tent was hastily pitched, and a folding cot placed in it so that the señorita might repose herself in it if she chose. There was a round dozen of these servants and, besides the animals they bestrode, there were fully twenty pack-mules which bore the necessities for the journey.

In this manner it will be seen how Torreño transformed a fifty-mile canter into a campaign. There were some three score and ten horses and mules; there were almost as many men. And the cavalcade stretched splendidly over many and many a rod of ground. There was a great jingling of little silver and golden bells. And the dust cloud flew into a great flag flying from beneath the many hoofs as they mounted each hilltop, and settled in a heavy, stifling fog around them as they lurched down into every hollow. They marched eight hours a day, and their average was hardly more than two miles an hour, counting the halts, and weary, slow labor up the many slopes. Therefore, it was a march of fully three days.

All of this had been foreseen by the omniscient Torreño. Accordingly, he had built three lodgings at the end of the three separate days' riding. Some flimsy structure, you would say, some fabric of wood and canvas? No, no! Such tawdry stuff was not for Torreño! He sent his adobe brickmakers and his builders ahead to the sites months before. He sent them not by the dozen, but by the score. They erected three spreading, solid build-ings. They cleared the ground around them. They constructed commodious sleeping apartments. And the foresters of Torreño brought down from the foothills of the snow-topped Sierras young pines and firs and planted them again around the various halting places, planted them in little groups, so that they made groves of shade, for the season of her arrival was a season of summer heat. And where in the world is the sun more burningly hot than in the great West of the Americas?

Shall it be said that these immense labors strained the powers of the rich Torreño? Not in the least! For the servants of the great man he numbered by whole villages and towns— Indians who had learned to live only to labor, and to labor only for their Spanish masters. He had almost forgotten the commands he had given until, riding down to the port, he had passed through the lodges one by one and, with the view of each, the heart of Torreño had swelled with pride. For the glory of his riches had never grown strange to Don Francisco. His father had been a moneylender in Barcelona who had raised his son in abject penury and left him, at his death, a more than modest competence. Don Francisco had loaned it forth again, at a huge interest, to a certain impoverished grandee, a descendant of one of those early conquistadores who considered the vast West of North America as their backyard. The grandee had been unable to pay interest. In short, in a year Don Francisco foreclosed and got for the larger half of his money—a whole kingdom of land. He sailed out to explore his possessions. For days he rode across it, league after league, winding up valleys with rich bottomlands, climbing well-faced mesas, struggling over endless successions of hills.

"What will grow here?" he asked in despair.

"Grass, señor, you see!"

They pointed out to him sun-cured grasses.

"But what will eat this stuff?"

"It is the finest food in the world for either cattle or horses," he was told.

He did not believe, at first. It was a principle with him never to believe except under the compulsion of his own eyes, but, when he extended his rides through the neighboring estates, he indeed found cattle, hordes of them—little, lean-bodied, wild-eyed creatures as fleet as antelope, as savage as tigers. They, indeed, could drink water once in three days and pick a living on the plains. So Don Francisco, half in despair, bought a quantity of them—they could be had almost for the asking— and turned them loose on his lands. He gave other attention to the bottomgrounds and farmed them with care, and at the end of ten years, his farmland was rich, to be sure, but the cattle had multiplied by miracle until they swarmed everywhere. Each one was not worth a great deal—nothing in compari- son with the sleek, grass-fed beeves which he remembered in old Spain, but they were numbered, as has been said, by the square league. They needed no care. They grew fat where goats would have starved. They multiplied like rabbits. In short, it took ten years for Don Francisco to awaken to the truth; then he got up one morning and found himself richer than his rich- est dreams of wealth. He went back to Spain, bought a palace in Madrid, hired a small army of servants, dazzled the eyes of the city, and, as a result, got him a wife of his own choosing, high-born, magnificent, loving his money, despising him. She bore him this one son, Don Carlos, and then died of a broken heart among the arid hills of America, yearning ever for the stir and the bustle and the whispers of Madrid. In the meantime, Don Francisco grew richer and richer. He began to buy his own ships and employ his own captains to transport the hides and the tallow back to Europe. He sent expeditions northward along the coast an incredible distance into the frozen regions, and they brought back furs by the sale of which alone he could have made himself the richest man in Barcelona. But he no longer thought of Barcelona. He thought of the world as his stage. When he thought of kingdoms and of kings, he thought of his own wide lands, and of himself in the next breath.

Such was Señor Don Francisco Torreño.

Now he had brought back from Spain another lovely girl, this time to become the wife of his son, Don Carlos. Men had told him that she was not only a d'Arquista, but that she was also the loveliest girl in all of Spain, and, although he had not believed the last, when he saw her now, swaying and tilting in the lumbering carriage like a very flower, he could not but agree that she was worthy to be a queen.

And was not that, in fact, the destiny for which he was shaping her? In the end he found that he could give her the highest compliment which it was in his power to bestow on any woman—she was worthy to be the wife of the son of Francisco Torreño!

As for Don Carlos, he was in a seventh heaven, an ecstasy of delight. He could not keep his eyes from touching on his bride-to-be, and, every time they rested on her, he could not help smiling and twirling the ends of his little mustaches into dagger points. He went to his father.

"Ah, sir," he said. "Where can I find words in the world to tell you of my gratitude? In all the kingdoms, you have found the one lady of my heart."

Torreño was pleased, but he would have scorned to show his pleasure.

"Bah!" he said. "You are young . . . therefore, you are a fool. Remember that she is a woman, and every woman is a confederacy of danger in your household. When the married man locks his door, he has not closed out from his house his deadliest foe!"

"I shall not believe that there is evil in her," said the youth. He clapped his hand upon the hilt of his rapier. He had been to Milan and to Paris to learn the proper use of that weapon, and, though some parts of his education might be at fault, in swordplay he had been admitted a master even by the Spaniards, who fight by rule of book like mathematicians, and even by the French who fight like dreadful angels of grace. "And," said Don Carlos, "if another man were to suggest such a thing, I should . . . cut his throat!"

His father was pleased again. He loved violence in his boy, just as he loved his elegance. In all things, Don Carlos was his ideal of what a young man should be, just as he himself was what his ideal of a man of sixty should be.

"You throat-cutters," said Don Francisco sneeringly. "Powder and lead are the only things!"

So saying, he snatched a pistol from the holster beside his saddle and, jerking it up level with his eye, fired. He had intended to shave the long plume which fluttered from the hat of one of his postilions. As a matter of fact, the ball knocked the hat off the head of the poor fellow, and even grazed his skull, so that he screamed with terror and clapped both hands to the top of his head.

"Indians!" shouted the driver.

"Indians!" echoed the rear guard and the front.

Instantly they faced out and held their carbines at the ready. Don Francisco was convulsed with laughter. He rolled back and forth in his saddle and waved his pistol in the air, helpless with excess of mirth.

"Ah," he groaned in his joy, "did you see the face of the fool, Carlos? Did you see?"

But Carlos was already at the side of the carriage, comforting his lady and assuring her that it was only a jest of his father's. She had not uttered an outcry, but she sat stiff and straight in the carriage and looked at her fiancé with a very strange expression in her eyes—a strange, level glance that went through and through the soul of Don Carlos like the cold steel of a rapier—and out again at a twitch.

"Ah," she said without a smile, "was that a joke? What if the man had been killed?"

"Why, there are a thousand others to take his place," explained Don Carlos carefully.

"I see," she said.

And that was all. But at that moment he would have given a very great deal if she had smiled even a very small smile.

II

In the confusion that followed the explosion of the gun, the carriage, as a matter of course, had come to a halt. It had stopped in the center of a deep hollow where the road, pounded repeatedly by the great wheels of the carts which brought the hides down to the seaport town, had been scored with great ruts, and the surface cut away to the undercrop of rocks. Against one of these, the rear wheels were wedged and, when the postilions tried to start the coach, they failed. They could not, at once, get the team to work together, partly, perhaps, because they were talking to one another—a rapid muttering running back and forth along the line of the drivers.

In the meantime, Señorita Lucia stood up and beckoned to her cavalier. He was in the midst of a rapture which he was pouring forth to his father.

"She is like a bird, sir," he was saying. "She is full of music. There is nothing about her that is not delightful."

"Bah!" said the father, concealing his happiness as usual with a scowl. "Take care that she does not prove a sparrow-hawk, and you the sparrow!"

"When I hear her voice, my heart stops. Her eyes take hold on my soul like a strong hand. I could wish for only one thing . . . that she would smile more often. Do you think that she is happy? That she will be happy?"

His father turned short around in his saddle.

"Is she a fool?" he asked. "Can she not see that this is my land? And that all that we are to journey through is my land? Are not the cattle mine, the trees mine, everything but the sky itself mine? Did she not eat from silver dishes yesterday? Does she not eat from golden dishes today? And yet you ask if she is happy? Carlos, that is the question of a madman!"

"But she seems thoughtful."

"All women," said his father, "think while they are young. There is a need for that. They use their brains until they have caught a husband. After that, their minds go to sleep. It is better so. Rather an unfaithful wife than a thinking wife! Such creatures give a man no rest. And in our homes we should have peace!"

So said the great Torreño, and then nodded. Since he cared for the opinion of no one else in the world, he found a great delight in agreeing with himself.

It was at this moment that the son saw his lady beckoning to him. He drove in the spurs so deep, in his haste, that the tortured horse leaped straight up into the air. But as well to have striven to unseat a centaur as to dispossess this master of the saddle. Presently, Don Carlos drew rein beside the coach, his horse sliding to a halt upon braced legs. But to the dismay of the gallant Don Carlos, he found that Señorita Lucia was not even looking at him. She was raising one hand as though for silence. Her head was lifted and there was an expression of perfect concentration on her face.

"Will you tell them to be quiet?" she asked him.

"Idiots!" cried he. "Fools! Will you be still? Will you be barking like wild dogs?"

He stormed up and down the line of the postilions. Each was transformed to stone, looking sullenly down upon the ground. He came back to Lucia smiling like a happy child. There was not a sound, now, except the heavy panting of the horses. The dust cloud rose and floated away on the slow wind. The sun beat steadily, burningly down upon them. It dried the sweat on the flanks of the horses as fast as it formed and left powderings of salt.

"Now," said the girl, "you can hear it quite clearly. I thought I heard before . . . now I am sure."

Don Carlos listened in turn, pointed the eye of his mind, so to speak, in the direction to which she pointed, and then he made out, very far and faint, very thin but very clear, like a star ray on a dark black night, the sound of a whistled music which floated to them through the air, now drowned by a stir of the wind, now coming again.

"That is a great flute player . . . that is a true musician," said the lady.

He gaped at her for a moment. Something that his father had said was recurring to his not overly alert brain. Indeed, this was very like the hawk which knew what duller fowl could not. How had she been able to pick up that liquid, tiny sound through the jingling, stamping, creaking, shouting of the caravan?

It made her seem tall—though she was very small. It made her eye like the eye of an eagle, though it was only of the mildest blue.

He was filled with awe, and with astonishment. He had never felt such an emotion before, not even in the presence of his father, of whom he was terribly afraid.

"Who is it?" asked the girl. "It must be a man famous in this part of the country."

He could not tell her. He shouted to his father. But Don

Francisco could not say who it might be. Neither did any of the others in the train have a guess to venture.

"I shall ride off to find him," said Don Carlos. "I shall be back in a moment."

"No," said the girl. "I shall go myself."

Among the led horses, of which there were half a dozen or more, there were two always kept saddled and ready for her in case she should choose to change from the carriage. She had not shown the slightest inclination to leave that lumbering vehicle before. Now, therefore, everyone watched with the greatest attention, and the silent eagerness of born horsemen, while she dismounted from the coach and stood before the two horses. One was a bay, beautiful as a picture, but a useless creature except for a gift of soft gaits. The other was a roan, ugly in color, but chosen because of its rare and eager spirit, combined with perfect manners, and a mouth as sensitive as the mouth of a human being.

"Let us see," said Don Francisco when those horses were selected for her special use, "if she can tell a horse from a horse. If she can do that, she can be happy in this wild country, even if she were the bride of a beggar!"

Now he rode close up.

"There is a right one and a wrong one," he said.

He took a ring from his finger. There was an emerald in it.

"You shall have this, my child, if you prove yourself wise."

She gave him a steady glance, once again without a smile. Then she turned back to the others and regarded their heads.

"Not their heads only," entreated Don Carlos, anxious that she might make a good impression upon his father. And of the two heads, that of the bay was far the more beautiful. "Look at the whole body . . . the legs . . . the bone . . . the hard muscle, Lucia."

She shrugged her shoulders. "I shall ride this one," she said, and laid her hand on the nose of the roan.

There was a little shout from the whole cavalcade. For she had run the gauntlet unscathed! But Don Francisco was almost scowling on her as he gave her the ring. And he muttered to his son: "A hawk. Poor Carlos."

Don Carlos did not quite follow the meaning that might be hidden away under this. He was too delighted by her victory. And, in another moment, she was galloping away at his side across the hills.

It was even farther than he had guessed, but the music led them across two ranges of the little rolling hills, and on the second range, they saw their man seated cross-legged under a tree, with the flute at his lips and his agile fingers dancing over it.

He was a tall man with a white band of cloth around his long, black hair to keep it away from his face, and clean white trousers which extended to his heels. There was a sash around his waist. Altogether he was a romantic figure in such a setting among the olive-drab hills.

"Look!" said Don Carlos, as they drew rein.

At their approach, the musician had jumped up and whistled sharply. And at once the sheep which were feeding in that pasture land came running toward him, a rush of gray white which pooled around his feet, bleating and babbling.

The Indian, as he arose, was revealed as a slender-waisted and broad shouldered man—with the form of an athlete and the air of a gravely reserved thinker.

"He looks," said the girl, "like a hero."

"He?" said Don Carlos. "He is only an Indian."

"He is not like the others," she said, looking thoughtfully at her fiancé.

"The others are mere root grubbers, ditch diggers," said the son of the lord of the land, shrugging his shoulders. "This fellow is different . . . yes. You can tell that he is a Navajo by that band around his hair and his white trousers. The Navajos are different. Most of them are men. But no Navajo with an ounce of blood in his veins would be herding sheep for a white man. This man is probably an outcast, a coward, perhaps a fool, certainly a knave!"

She gave Don Carlos one look, a long one; she gave the Indian another glance, a short one.

"I don't agree with you," she said.

"Why not, Lucia?"

"Because he is a musician. That's one thing. And besides . . ."

"Besides what?"

"I don't know," she said, and added: "Talk to him, Carlos."

This was pronounced so shortly that Don Carlos stared a little, for he had never in his life received commands except from his father who, after all, was a sort of deity of another order. However, when he looked to the girl, he found her smiling so frankly that he quite forgot he had received an order.

Now he reined his horse closer. The Indian had folded his hands and addressed his gaze to the distant mountains, lofty, naked rock faces, spotted richly with color all dim and blended behind a veiling mist.

"Tell me, fellow," said Don Carlos, "what is your name?"

He had asked the question, of course, in Spanish, and the Indian returned to him a dull, unintelligent stare.

"I shall ask him in Navajo," said Don Carlos to the girl. "He has probably come here only newly. Otherwise he would have understood such a simple question. These Navajos, besides, are not such fools, you know."

He said to the Indian, in a broad, quick guttural: "What is your name? Quickly, because we cannot stay here. What is your name, and what made you learn the flute?"

Not a whit of intelligence glimmered in the steady black eyes of the other. Don Carlos flushed.

"The oaf dares to keep silent!" he said. "I shall give him a lesson that will be written in his skin the rest of his life!"

And he raised a riding whip. At the same instant, into the hand of the Indian came a long and heavy knife. He did not hold it by the hilt, but balanced it loosely in the palm of his hand, the knife blade extending over the fingers, so that it was plain he intended to throw it, and there was something in his unmoved air which gave assurance that his weapon would not miss the target. Don Carlos, with a gasp of rage and astonishment, whirled his horse away.

"The scoundrel!" he cried. "We'll silence that flute, by heaven! Turn your face, Lucia!"

"Carlos!" she cried, riding straight between him and his intended target. "Do you mean to pistol him in cold blood?"

"Cold blood?" cried he. "I tell you, Lucia, if we did not keep these desert rats down, they would eat through our walls and knife us in our sleep. They'd swarm over the whole land. There is only one way to treat an Indian . . . like a mad dog!"

Her expression, for the moment, reminded him of that of the Navajo—it was the blank of one who veils a thought.

"Here comes your father," she said. "Perhaps he will speak for Señor Torreño."

Torreño, in fact, had followed the two at a slow gait, not close enough to interfere with their privacy, but at a sufficient distance to keep his eye upon them, as though he dared not risk the safety of the two human beings who meant the most to him in the world.

III

He had no sooner come up when his son explained everything that had happened in the following way:

"I asked this Indian dog for his name in Spanish and in Navajo. He dared to remain silent."

"So?" said Torreño. "A Navajo, however, is not a dog, but a man . . . or half a man." He said gently to the tall Indian: "Amigo, do you know me?"

Instantly, the other made answer in perfect Spanish, smooth, close-clipped, the truest Castilian: "You are my master, señor! You are Señor Torreño."

Torreño turned to the girl with a broad grin on his face, as much as to say: "This you see is another matter when the right man speaks!"

He added to the Indian. "And now your name?"

"I am Taki, the son of . . ."

"That is enough. So, Taki, you have drawn a knife upon my son?"

"A knife?" said Taki blankly. "I cannot remember that!"

The girl broke into ringing laughter, a small, sweet voice in the vast silence of those hills. The music of it softened the hard heart of Torreño.

"I should have had him flayed alive," he said. "But since he has amused you, dear girl, I shall forgive him."

"Flayed alive?" murmured the girl. "Are such things possible here?"

"In this country," said Torreño, "one must be a king or a slave . . . and to be a king, one must be a tyrant. I, señorita, am a tyrant, partly because it is necessary, partly because it pleases me to be one. Where I am, there is no other word, except for the sake of conversation."

He said this with a grave, sharp glance at her, which could not avoid giving the words a certain meaning. Whether she understood or not, however, could not be seen, for again her face wore an expression as grave and as unreadable as the Indian's. Torreño turned back to the culprit.

"You have drawn a knife upon my son . . . who is my flesh, who is me. Would you strike steel into my arm?"

"Heaven forbid, señor."

"This Don Carlos is more than my arm. He is part of my heart. He is that part of me which will live after my death. To touch him is to touch me."

He added an aside to the girl: "That is rather neatly spoken, child, is it not?"

"A pretty speech," said she without emotion.

"Señor, my master," said the Indian.

"Well?" queried Torreño.

"I have a horse, señor."

"You are rich, then? But what of the horse?"

"He is mine. He is my slave."

"Ah?"

"When I whistle, he comes. When I speak, he lifts his ears. I need no bridle to control him."

"This fellow," said Torreño, "talks like a man of sense . . . if I could only understand what he is striking at."

This was spoken, like the rest of his asides, in French. And the Navajo instantly answered for himself, in the purest French of Paris, where alone French was pure.

"I mean that the horse is my slave, señor."

"By the heavens!" broke out Torreño. "The fellow speaks French, also. Better French than I use myself!"

"Wait, wait!" said the girl in a hurried voice, raising her hand to stop interruptions, and staring fixedly at the Indian. "He has something more to say."

"Aye," said Torreño, nodding. "The horse is your slave."

"Because he will do these things," said the Indian, "and because he is fleeter than the horses, even, which you ride, señor . . ."

"What! That's a broad lie, Taki!"

At this, the other stiffened a little.

"Nevertheless," he said, "it is true. It is a fleeter horse than any of those you ride. And it is also my slave. But, señor, though I value him more than gold, it is because his speed is all for me. His strength is all mine. No other man can sit on his back. To them, he is a devil."

"You are right, Taki. That is something I can understand."

"If he were a horse for any man to ride, I should not care. There would be a price upon him. But me he serves for love! Therefore, he is priceless."

"Very well . . . very well. And what has this to do with the knife you drew on my son, the Señor Don Carlos Torreño? By the heavens, Taki, tell me that."

"If a man were to take a whip to that horse of mine, señor, should I not be happy if he used his heels?"

Passion had been swelling in the face, in the throat of Torreño. Now it relaxed a little.

"I begin to understand. I begin to understand. You, Taki, will have only one master?"

"Señor, you have spoken."

"Not even if I assign you to another by express command?"

"Not even then, señor."

"God!" thundered the Spaniard. "There is a hangman and a rope for disobedient slaves!"

"Señor," said Taki, "death is half a second . . . but every day of slavery is a century of hell."

"Ten thousand devils," said Torreño. "He talks like a fool!"

"Or a philosopher," said the girl, "and still more . . . like a brave man!"

"But are you not," said Torreño, "at this moment in my service?"

"For another fortnight, only."

"What?"

"It is true."

"Taki, are you mad?"

"No, señor."

"I employ no man except when he is bought or hired for life."

"To me, however, you made an exception."

"In what manner? Have I ever seen you before?"

"There was a crossing of a river," said the other. "A dozen men were riding after one Indian. They shot his horse. He swam the river. They followed, swimming their horses. He killed the first man ashore with his knife, took his horse, and rode on. But the horse was tired. The others behind him gained. He was not ten minutes from death by fire, señor, when he saw you and your party and rode to you and . . ."

"I remember, I remember!" cried Torreño, clapping

his hands together. "It is all as clear as the ringing of a bell. I remember it all! You came to us with Pedro Marva and his hired fighters raging and foaming behind you. I put in, between. They were very hot, but not so hot that they did not know me. Ha?"

"They knew you, señor," said the Indian gravely.

Don Carlos was gaping at this story, but Señorita Lucia flushed and bit her lip.

"They knew me," went on Torreño, "and when I told them that they could not have the man . . . because his riding pleased me . . . they turned around and went off, cursing. However, I paid Marva for his dead man . . . and all was well!"

"It's true . . . it is very true," said the Indian.

"You paid for the life of a man? A white man?" asked the girl.

"All things have a price . . . in this country," said the Spaniard.

She did not answer, but she looked around her on the bald, vast sweep of plain and mountain. She looked up, and there were tiny, circling dots which ruled the sky—the buzzards. And she shuddered a very little.

"But how," said the Spaniard, "are you to be in my service only a fortnight longer? I remember it all. You were to serve me until you had paid for the price of the man. And twelve hundred pesos could not be worked out in ten lives of a shepherd. How have you made the money?"

"There are more than eleven hundred pesos," said the Navajo, "already in the hands of your treasurer. He has kept the account. I have the rest to pay in soon."

"Rascal!" said the Spaniard. "You have not been in my service for six months."

"Señor, there are ways of making money, even for a poor shepherd."

"Who leaves his sheep?"

"Only at night, when a friend will come to watch them."

"Ah? Ah? You are a worker by night, Taki? And what do you find at night?"

"There was a great rider of the roads. There was a Captain Sandoval . . ."

"He was killed three months ago. What of him? I was away."

"There was a reward on his head."

"Of five hundred pesos. Yes."

"The reward was paid to me, señor."

"The devil fly off with me! The terrible Sandoval . . . and one Indian killed him? How in the name of heaven?"

The Indian turned. His hand flashed back and forward. A line of light left it and went out in the trunk of a narrow sapling, which shivered with the shock. There stood the knife, buried to the hilt in the hard wood.

"Name of heaven," whispered Don Carlos, and touched his heart, as though just there he felt the resistless death slide in.

"Ah?" said Torreño. "It was in that way?"

"It was in that way."

"And he did not touch you?"

"His pistol bullet just touched my hair, señor."

"That accounts for five hundred pesos only."

"There was another . . . a friend of Sandoval. Some said it was his younger brother, and he was a greater man . . . There were six hundred pesos on his head. That money became mine."

"Now I remember that it was said an Indian killed poor Juan Sandoval. But it was you, Taki? I am growing old . . . Things happen on this place, and I do not know of them! Still, Taki, that leaves a hundred pieces of silver. How have you saved them?"

"There are the dice, señor."

"A head hunter, a gambler . . ." began Don Carlos.

"And a musician," said the girl. "In what way did you learn to play the flute, Taki?"

"Señor Arreto, a great Spaniard, came to fight against my people. I was wounded and captured. But in the fighting he watched me and thought I was worth keeping . . . as a slave. He took me back to Europe with him. It was amusing, señorita, to see the poor Indian learn to dance, to play the flute, to bow, and to talk like a real man. So I was taught. I went with him among fine people. When people talked of his journeys, he pointed to me. It proved that he was a great hunter. Imagine, señorita, a hunter come back from India with a tamed tiger in his company to follow at his heels like a dog."

This ironical speech was so delivered that neither Torreño nor his rather dull son quite caught the point of it, but the girl smiled faintly.

"And so you learned to play the flute?"

"Yes, señorita. My day was divided in three parts. There was the fencing master, the dancing master, the music master. In the afternoons I was taken forth and shown to the people. Everyone wished to hear me play the flute. Now and then a brave lady who was not too proud permitted me to dance with her. And twice bravos were hired to fight with me and prove what I had learned from the fencing masters."

"And . . . ?"

"I killed them both, señorita."

"Then what followed?"

"When Señor Arreto died, he gave me my liberty. I took my little money and bought a certain fine horse which I had seen. The price was low, because the horse was a tiger and would not be tamed. But I, who had been tamed, understood how to manage him. With that horse I returned to this country."

"One instant, Taki," broke in Don Carlos, raising his hand

and delighted to make a point. "If you are a master of the sword, why would you hunt your head . . . with a knife?"

"The teeth which God gives us," said the Indian, bowing, "are better than false ones for eating, señor."

"What do you think of him?" asked Torreño of the girl.

"He is enchanting," she whispered back.

"An enchanting liar!" he said. "There never was an Indian in the world who could manage a weapon so formal as a sword. Shall I prove it?"

"If it can be done."

"Ride back," said Torreño to his son, "and bring two foils. Quickly."

There was no need for the last word. All commands of Torreño implied the necessity for speed, and Don Carlos was instantly rushing back at the full flight of his horse toward that waiting caravan.

The girl drew closer to Torreño.

"For the little time that remains for him to serve you," she said, "let me have this man for a servant."

"He will not be alive in ten minutes," said Torreño. "You will see that he handles the sword like a fool. And when that happens, I intend to shoot that liar down like the dog that he is. No Indian can kill a white, even a villainous white, and remain a good Indian!"

She grew pale, started to speak, then changed her mind and said simply: "But if he fences well?"

"That is impossible!"

"But?"

"Then he is yours, but give the dog a muzzle!"

IV

Don Carlos came back at full speed, as he had gone, and he brought with him two foils in their scabbards, with leather covers over the hilts. Torreño took them, unbuckled the flaps which secured the hilts, and drew forth the blades. One by one, he whipped them through the air until they sang.

"Most people," he said to the girl, "use for their foils dull iron things, or poor steel that bends to nothing after a strong touch or two. But these are of the finest old Spanish steel, specially made for my boy in order that he might have exercise."

Her face lighted a little. "You love to fence, then, señor?"

"I? Love it? The devil take it. One good broad sword is worth a dozen such great darning needles, I say, or a saber at least. I have seen a Pole use a saber that it would have done your eyes good to watch him, but this stamping and parading and retreating and advancing and sweating and bowing and scraping . . . bah! It makes me laugh to see it. When one good pistol bullet would put an end to it all!"

The light which had flickered into her eyes went out again.

"Here, Carlos," he said to his son. "Take one of these."

"For what, sir?" asked the son.

"Taki says that he's a fencer. If he can touch you . . . well, he is. If he cannot . . . he is a dead Indian."

He drew out a huge horse pistol as he spoke and flourished it.

"Do you hear me, Taki?"

"Yes."

"Do you agree?"

"It is to see if I have lied about the fencing lessons," said the Navajo. "It is very just."

"Señor!" cried the girl. "You do not mean it!"

"Peace, Lucia," said Torreño, bending his brows upon her. "Peace, child. Do not question the workings of my mind. You are a bright little thing, Lucia. But do not trot your wits over the same trail that I follow. For that is dangerous, and I would not abide it. I live alone, my girl. I live alone, I promise you. I open my purposes to whom I please. And to those who do not please me, I keep them closed. And so . . . for that!"

The girl had turned white. But she kept her eyes on the ground, while poor Don Carlos looked upon her in an agony, aching to comfort her or to speak a word to her, but not daring to move or to speak. He merely accepted the foil from the hand of his father and automatically stood en garde.

"Now, let me see," said Torreño, with a serene brow, as if he had already forgotten the manner in which he had trod roughshod over the girl, "let me see you work for your life, Taki, for your life. Liars are usually interesting people . . . but not when they're Indians. A truthful Indian or a dead one is my motto. Come! Engage!"

The blades crossed as he spoke, and Don Carlos, impatient to have the dirty work over with, with a curl of fine disdain on his lip as he faced his humble opponent, put the other's blade sharply aside and, continuing his point in the same motion, lunged full home. That is to say, he drove straight at the heart of the Indian, and the latter opposed no guard, yet managed to escape the button of the Spaniard by a supple bending of his body.

"You see?" said Torreño to the girl. "The fool knows nothing of the sword. The knife is as far as his brute heart can aspire."

"He is a musician, señor," said the girl. "This ring you have given me against . . . his service to me . . . that he wins."

The other gaped at her. "Win, Lucia? Win? Are you mad? No, he is as good as dead already!"

"Nevertheless," she said, "though I ask your pardon for denying you, he is a fine fencer. See!"

Don Carlos, angered by the first lack of fortune, pressed hotly in, following lunge with thrust and thrust with lunge. But the Indian, still parrying only a little, escaped the point still by constantly retreating and by the deftness of his footwork.

"Any fool can run away from trouble," said Don Francisco. "Taki, Taki, I wish to see fencing, not a footrace. Stand to him . . ."

He had not finished off his oath at his leisure when Taki stopped, indeed seemed to flick aside the blade of Don Carlos, and instantly dipped his own blade at Don Carlos. Then he leaped back and lowered his foil.

"A touch!" cried the girl. "He has won!"

"Seven thousand devils!" groaned Torreño. "Carlos . . . idiot . . . have you allowed him . . . ?"

"I hardly felt it . . . I am sure it was not a touch," panted Don Carlos. "It could not have been a touch."

"I saw his foil bend as the button touched you, Carlos," said the girl coldly.

"He did not feel it . . . I did not see it!" exclaimed the tyrant. "It was not a touch! Engage!"

Don Carlos made a strange gesture to the girl, as though disclaiming this lack of sportsmanship. Then he hurried to cross swords with Taki. The latter showed not the slightest disappointment or excitement. But he was a little more gravely watchful as he engaged. Neither was Don Carlos so impetuous. He had been foolishly hasty before. He summoned all of his care at this moment, and he was not only the product of the finest teaching in the world, but he was a credit to that teaching.

But to the amazement of them all, Taki now stood his ground without flinching, putting aside the lunges and the thrusts of Don Carlos with the most consummate ease and, at the same time, so fluid were his own movements that he was able to talk, slowly, but without panting.

"I am forbidden to retreat, señor," he said to Don Carlos. "Therefore, you will forgive me if I stand my ground for an instant before you. As for the last touch, it was upon your belt, and it was for that reason that you did not feel it, I have no doubt. The next time, with ten thousand pardons, I shall try to lodge the button against your throat . . . against the hollow of your throat, señor, if I can be so fortunate, for the sake of making that touch an unmistakable one. You will forgive me for it, señor?"

"Why, curse you," said Don Carlos through his teeth as he worked, "that time will never come!"

"Look!" cried the girl. "Look!"

It was, indeed, a strange sight to watch the Indian. A slight wind had come up and blew his long hair back from his head, showing that lean face to greater advantage. And there was still the same quiet, thoughtful expression in his eyes. His head canted a little to one side, as though his opponent were at a distance. His look was rather that of a gunner than a swordsman. Only, from time to time, his foil was a wall of the most solid steel against which the assaults of Don Carlos clashed noisily but could not break through.

Then: "Señor, a thousand, ten thousand pardons, as they say in Paris. But . . . there is a necessity."

And he attacked. For an instant Don Carlos bore up against the attack like a swimmer against a turning tide. Then he was borne back while his father shouted in a rage.

"Is this the result of the money I have spent on you? Oh, fool! Oh, dolt! I wish to heaven that the Indian's point was unbated! I wish it were through your heart! I have a lump, a clod for a son! Oh, what a shame this is to me! It is an Indian, not a gentleman who stands before you, Carlos! Are you sleeping? And if . . ."

His voice broke off short. The button of the Navajo at that instant lodged against the throat of Carlos with such force that the strong blade of the foil doubled up like a supple switch in his hand. Carlos dropped his sword, caught at his throat, and then sank gasping to the ground.

It was Taki who raised him first. But he received across the body a slashing stroke from the riding whip of Torreño, who instantly flung himself from his horse and caught his son in his arms.

"Carlos!" he cried. "Is it well with you? You are not hurt? I shall kill him if your skin is so much as broken! If . . ."

Carlos recovered speech with a groan.

"He is the finest fencer in the world. Father, this is no Indian. Or else he is a devil disguised." He added: "Let him alone. Don't harm him. I had rather know that last trick than have a million pesos!"

"You have had the finest blades in Milan and Paris to teach you. You come home to me to take lessons from a Navajo? You have my flesh and my blood in you. Otherwise, Carlos, I should call you a fool outright. Lucia, that man is yours!"

He mounted his horse and rode furiously away.

"He will never forgive me," said Don Carlos sadly, still fingering his throat. "As for you, Taki," he said, turning a black scowl upon the Indian, "I'll teach you to curse this day!"

The Indian smiled. And there was more scorn in that smile than in a torrent of wordy abuse.

Don Carlos stormed like a leashed dog: "You red-skinned snake!"

"Señor," said the Indian, "I belong now to the lady . . . and as her servant I dare not submit to such words. Our swords were bated, señor. But I have a second knife which is not."

"Carlos," said the girl, "don't speak with him again. Taki, you must leave the sheep where they are. You must follow us. You have a horse which you love too much to keep far away from you. Where is it now?"

"Waiting, señorita."

"Bring, it then."

He whistled high and shrill as the scream of a hawk, and then, as they waited, they heard a rush of hoofs, and a shining bay stallion whipped into view. He came up with the wind and the sun rippling in his mane and in his tail. At the side of Taki he paused, tossing up his head and snorting at the strangers.

"Saddle and bridle him," said the girl, "if you can. He is a glorious thing, Taki. I have never seen such a beauty . . . not in the king's stables!"

"He is saddled," said Taki, throwing a blanket over the back of the stallion and securing it with a single cinch. And, fastening a light halter of thin rawhide over his head: "He is bridled," he added.

"Then come after us," said the girl. "You have a fortnight of service remaining, Taki. That fortnight belongs to me!"

V

The apartment of Lucia in the rest house, which the cavalcade reached, was like that in which she had spent her first night after leaving the ship, except that it was, perhaps, a little more complete. She herself went about restlessly examining everything. But she said not a word. It was her aunt, the pale and patient lady who had chaperoned her niece to this far land, who broke forth into eulogy and into wonder.

"It is like a scene from some biblical story, Lucia," she declared, "illustrated in the concrete. What a wonderful and strange country this is!"

"A wonderful and strange Francisco Torreño," said the girl without emotion.

Her own chambers consisted of a large room at a corner of the house, with two small, deep windows cut through each wall; in those casement recesses were small climbing vines whose roots extended to the outside of the wall, where they were sunk in pots of rich, wet soil. There were chairs and couches, crudely made but cushioned to softness and everywhere—on chairs, on couches, on the floor beneath their feet—were fine sheepskins washed to a dazzling whiteness, and combed until they were light as a mist before the face of the moon. To the side of this chamber in one direction were two small bedchambers, each well-nigh filled with gigantic four-posters, one for Lucia and one for her aunt, Anna d'Arquista. On the other side of her reception room were two other apartments to correspond with the sleeping rooms. One was the bath; the other was a small chapel. In the making of the bath alone, a very world of labor had been expended, for in digging the foundation for the house, the builders had struck a solid rock, dark green like seawater. This had been chiseled out to an appropriate depth and little steps cut in the side, so that the lady Lucia might walk down into her bath. The remainder of the floor of the bathroom was paved with great slabs of red limestone, soft and yet porous, delicate to the touch of a bared foot. And there was a red sandstone bench made of three large pieces of stone, roughly shaped but with a polished sitting surface. Into this room the servants were now bringing the heated water—an endless chain of dark-faced Indian women with earthen jars of water poised on their shoulders pacing gracefully in, each with a white flash of the eye as she passed the Señorita Lucia d'Arquista, seeing in her, indeed, the future empress who would control their destinies.

There are few who do not care to make their first impression an agreeable one, particularly to those who are socially inferior. But the señorita was one of the few. If there were kindness, gentleness in her heart, she carefully disguised it. If she looked at that passing line, it was in a detached, impersonal manner, as one might look at a painting.

And each of the serving women went on with a downcast glance fixed upon the brown heels of the one who went before. And the bath was gradually filled, each earthen jar discharging

a crystal stream of heated water into the bath where it was
turned instantly into pale green.

Last of all came two young girls, olive-skinned,
solemn-eyed, graceful as young trees in a wind as they
walked, strong as panthers, beautiful as evening. They passed
into the room of the bath. They took from small wooden
boxes handfuls of a powder which they dropped into the
quivering surface of the water; instantly a delicate fragrance
stole through the chambers, not to be identified, languor-
ously sweet as the perfume which a warm and lazy spring
wind gathers from a whole field of mingled wild flowers.
Then they came back before Lucia. They were sent by the
master, they said, and they were to prepare the señorita for
the bath, if it was her pleasure.

She spoke not to them but to her aunt in quick French:
"You see, madame, that one does not live in this country . . .
one is to be carried through life by slaves."

She turned her back and went to the door of the little
chapel.

"Hush, Lucia!" said Anna d'Arquista in the same language.
"Hush, child. One cannot tell what ears will hear you."

"Ah, yes," said the girl, without turning to answer, "you
feel it, also. Even the empty air has ears and is spying on us.
But look, madame, how this man who does not know a prayer
has fitted up a chapel for me."

It was complete. There was a jeweled crucifix. There was
a little gilded Madonna holding a child whose tiny hand was
raised to teach. There was a tall, pointed window filled with
stained glass beyond price. On the floor before the Madonna
was the skin of a great mountain lion. A strange prayer rug!

Anna d'Arquista came to look.

"All this," she said, "for a single night's resting place!

What a miracle of wealth . . . What a king this Torreño is! And who knows, Lucia? There may be a religious reverence in his heart, also."

"A religious fiddlesticks," said Lucia. "If a man has jewels, he shows them, does he not? All that he cares for in this place is the cost of making it. Look in the bath! How many hand strokes to make it . . . for this one evening only, perhaps!"

"It is wonderful, Lucia."

"Aye," said the girl, turning suddenly and throwing out her hands, "and beautiful, too. If one may be a queen, even over barbarians, why not?"

She went toward her bedroom, and the two attendants followed with stony faces. And poor Anna d'Arquista sank into a chair and laid her head in her hands and wept. For she loved her niece with all her heart, having mothered her, or tried to, for ten years. But where was all this swelling discontent in the girl pointing? To disaster, she felt, but disaster of what sort she hardly knew. It was a wretched business, she felt, and had always felt since the moment Lucia had been sold to this stranger from a strange land, sold not because the head of the d'Arquista family lacked money or lacked power, but because he was avaricious of more.

A curtain had been drawn across the bedroom door. Behind it she could hear voices—that of Lucia, like a small crystal bell, and then the soft, husky tones of the half-breed girls. They came out. The masks of stone had fallen from the attendants. They were smiling. Their happy eyes watched over their mistress as she walked a little before them, wrapped in a robe of blue silk, delicately brocaded. They entered the bath, the curtain was drawn, and then out to Anna d'Arquista floated noises of splashing water, and laughter sweet as the singing of birds—laughter from three throats!

Oh, to be young, thought Anna d'Arquista. What a miracle! What a miracle of grace and gracious power!

And to be beautiful! What virtue of a saint could balance against that gift? Aye, what could be surer of heaven itself, in the end? She pressed her cold, thin hands over her heart, because the ache in it made her faint.

Then, stealthily, she slipped into the chapel. She kneeled on the tawny lion skin. She rested her forehead against the altar of red limestone, and she prayed, or tried to pray. Afterward, she went back into the room, but time had hurried past her more quickly than she knew. That bath was ended; Lucia had been dressed; all the weariness of the day had been smoothed from her face; her eyes were filled with a reckless light.

"Find Taki," she said to the servants. "Send him to me."

They were gone instantly, hurrying to the door; then, as it closed behind them, the scurry of their running feet was faintly heard as they raced to be first in filling this command of their new mistress.

"They are sweet children," said Lucia.

Such a child to speak with love and with pity of children! And yet, to be sure, there was always something old in her niece. There was always a power of knowledge which made even Anna d'Arquista feel sometimes like a foolish infant.

Another step came to the door, and a hand knocked once.

"That is Taki," said the girl, her face brightening. "You have heard me tell about him. You have not seen him yet. When he comes in, watch his steps. They are like a tiger's. As swift, as strong, as noiseless. He is a dreadful creature, Aunt Anna!"

She called: "Come!"

The door opened; Taki glided in before them. There he stood in front of the closed door, his arms folded across his breast, his eyes upon the floor submissively—but it was the submission of a trained lion which passes through attitudes that have no meaning in its heart.

"Look," Lucia whispered. "He is magnificent, is he not?"

"And terrible," breathed the other.

He seemed larger, indeed, than he had before. Among the open hills, he fitted more easily into the picture. Here he seemed inches taller, stronger. Where his arms were folded, the muscles bulged beneath the sleeves of his shirt.

"You have come quickly, Taki," she said.

"I have been waiting," he said.

"You knew that I would send?"

"Yes, mistress."

She paused a moment, thoughtfully.

"That word, Taki," she said, "comes awkwardly from you, I think."

"I have been a free man . . . mistress," he said.

"Do you think that my service will be very hard?" she asked him.

"Ah," he said, with a stern smile touching his lips, "even to be the slave of a man is a knife in the heart of a slave."

She started at this.

"I think," she said to Anna d'Arquista, "that the rascal is impertinent!"

"Hush! Peace!" gasped out Anna d'Arquista. "If you rouse him, he will murder us both, crash through the wall, and escape."

Lucia d'Arquista laughed, but she shivered, also, and seemed to find that thrill of dread not unpleasant.

"And to serve a woman, any woman," she said, "is infinitely worse than to serve the worst of men?"

He remained silent.

"Did you hear me, Taki?"

He said at last: "Why should I speak when your answer is already in your own mind?"

And his eyes, for the first time, flashed up from the floor and looked into her own, not with a fleeting glance, but steadily, quietly.

VI

It made the lady frown, and then it made her flush. As for Aunt Anna, she was covered with terror.

"You are terribly unwise, my dear," she whispered to her niece.

But Lucia merely waved such fears aside with a graceful gesture.

"You don't understand," she said. "And I think that I do . . . a little."

This rather mysterious speech there was no time to explain.

"How long," said Lucia, "were you in Europe?"

"A year and two months, madame."

"A year and two months?" echoed Lucia.

Then she leaned back in her chair and began to smile like one who has solved a difficulty. She nodded at him again.

"One can easily see," she said, "how you could afford to spend so long a time on your studies."

He regarded her rather anxiously but did not speak.

"A year and two months," said Lucia, "completed your liberal education. Well, well, it is delightful to hear of such natural talents. There are some men who labor all their lives to learn how to fence, and even then they succeed only poorly. I remember that my father, even when he was quite an old man, used to spend an hour every day with the professor. He still takes fencing lessons twice a week. And I have a brother who has dreamed of nothing since he was a boy except to manage a rapier. But you, Taki, in the course of a year and two months, have reached such a point of skill that neither my father nor my brother could compare with you. I have seen them . . . I am sure that Señor Don Carlos Torreño fences as well as they do. And indeed, Don Carlos has made it the greatest work of his life . . . his fencing, I mean. It shows a very real and a very rare talent, Taki, that you have been able to learn so much in a short year and two months. You must have practiced very hard constantly."

He was still watching her with a shade of anxiety, but he answered: "I was constantly at work, señorita."

"But I forget! I forget! In that time you had also your lessons in dancing, in which I suppose you progressed as well as you did in fencing? Perhaps . . . even better?"

"I became a very stupid and very poor dancer, señorita."

She laughed at him. "Will you tell me that when you confess that the ladies would dance with you?"

"They were curious, señorita, to see the poor barbarian act like a civilized man."

"Nonsense!" she exclaimed, with the surety of absolute knowledge. "No woman would make herself appear ridiculous for the sake of curiosity. Not in such circles."

His face was covered instantly with his habitual mask.

"However, the dancing and the fencing is not all. By no means. There is the singular purity of your French, Taki. Most strange that one should pick up so perfect an accent in a single year. I, for instance, have worked half my life like a slave to learn that language. And still, any child could excel me! Indeed, Taki, you are very apt. You shame my father, my brother, Don Carlos, and me . . . You excel us so very far, Taki."

He answered with neither word nor look but still stared past her with a sort of bland indifference.

"But I have forgotten the most important thing of all," she exclaimed, "and the surest proof that you are a genius, Taki! You were able to master the flute in a single year . . . master it to a perfect smoothness. In a single year . . . that difficult instrument. In a single year, Taki, to become a master flute player, a dangerous and polished fencer, a dancer of grace at least . . . in a single year you have equipped yourself also with the very French of Paris. What additional study was there required to add Spanish to that list, for I see that you speak it with great precision. And," she added with a sudden change of voice, and speaking in excellent English, "what other languages are you a master of besides your own Navajo?"

"Of none, señorita," he answered, and then caught himself and bit his lip.

"You answer me in Spanish," she said, "but you understand the question I put in English."

"When I was a boy," said Taki, "I knew a trader who was from the colony of Virginia. I learned English from him."

She merely smiled, her eyes bright and hard as she examined him.

"Admirable, Taki," she said. "In all things you are excellent, in all things! Perhaps when you were a boy, you also knew a missionary who taught you French, a generous soldier who instructed you in fencing, a kind Spaniard who schooled you in Spanish grammar, and some dapper dancing master who went among the Navajos to teach them ballroom steps in their spare moments. So you had received the basis of your knowledge and the year in Paris was merely to add the perfect finish to what you already knew."

He did not reply, standing tall and stiff before her. There was no trace of emotion in him, except that the muscles of his folded arms swelled and rippled.

"That is all," she said. "You may go now."

He vanished instantly.

"Lucia, Lucia!" said her aunt. "I would never have dreamed of it. But you seemed to have proved that he has told us a great series of lies! Of course in one year he never could have accomplished what he claims."

Lucia was walking up and down the room, a faint smile on her lips. She did not answer at once.

"But the first thing is to tell Señor Torreño!" said Anna d'Arquista.

"Do you know what the señor would do?" asked the girl.

"Punish him, of course."

"Punish him by stripping him naked, giving him a start of a hundred paces, and then loosing the hounds after him! I heard him tell how he occasionally disciplines unfaithful servants."

"He is a stern man, indeed," said the elderly lady.

"If he were not so rich, he would not be called merely stern!"

"Lucia, what are you saying?"

"What I think."

"Oh, my dear, how dreadful!"

"To say what I think?"

"No, but I mean . . ."

"That I should not think? Yes, that is right. I should close my eyes. I should learn how to smile blindly. That would be the best, of course. It is sinful to see that he who is to be my father-in-law is brutal, savage, conceited, narrow."

"Lucia!"

"And it is a greater sin to guess that the gallant Don Carlos is a mere fool!"

"Ah, Lucia, God forgive me for listening to you. Child, child, what are you saying?"

"Nothing, nothing, of course. Nothing that should be remembered. I am preparing myself to be blind and deaf the rest of my life." She added sharply: "Because of this marriage, how many new estates will my father be able to buy, Aunt Anna? Can you guess that?"

Aunt Anna turned gray with horror and with dread. And her niece turned the subject.

"No," she said, "I shall give poor Taki a better start than Señor Torreño would give him. By this time the bay stallion has whipped him away toward the mountains faster than any wolf could run. Well, I trust that he rides well and fast and far. He is a strange man, Aunt Anna. Did you see the shadow over those black eyes of his when I showed him that I understood? Not a muscle of his face changed . . . except once."

"Ah, Lucia, he may do some terrible thing if you do not warn the Señor Torreño. I fear that this Taki has come with us for some purpose that is not good . . . Now that he is gone, I begin to be terribly afraid of him. When he was here . . . well, it was as though the skin of the mountain lion had come to life and the great beast lay crouched in the chapel, watching us with burning eyes. Chills and shudders went through me while Taki was in the room, here."

"And through me," said the girl, but she smiled.

"What will you do now?"

"Wait another five minutes."

"And then? Tell the señor?"

Lucia, instead of answering, dropped into a chair and began to study the changing light through the windows. The sky beyond was turning to a deeper blue as the sunset time came nearer. The minutes passed with Aunt Anna turning in her mind all that her niece had actually said and all that she had inferred. She dared not carry what she guessed to an actual conclusion. All that she knew was that her mind was full of confusion and dread of what would come of this unhappy marriage.

Lucia rose presently.

"It is time," she said. "He should be two leagues away by this time. If he is not . . ."

There was a little bronze bell standing on a polished table in the corner of the room. She struck it with the padded mallet which lay beside it, and one of her two attendants appeared at once.

"Find Taki," she commanded.

In two minutes the messenger appeared again.

"He is here," she said. "Shall I bring him in?"

"He is here?" breathed the girl.

"In the patio."

She slipped to the window and looked out. There stood Taki, the ruddy light from the west in his face, his expression as woodenly impassive as ever.

"Tell him," she said, "to wait there."

The servant bowed and left.

"Oh, Lucia?" breathed the other.

"I have told him that I know he is a liar," said Lucia. "And since he dares to stay . . . what Torreño does to him is on his own head. But what can his purpose be in remaining? What is in his barbarous mind, Aunt Anna?"

"God alone can read their thoughts . . . these solemn Indians," said Anna d'Arquista. "Perhaps he intends to murder us all while we're asleep and carry . . . our scalps . . . ah! You must send to Señor Torreño at once!"

"Yet," murmured the girl, "what a dull place this would be with the wild man gone. What a dull place. Hush! What is that?"

A thin thread of whistling, carrying a weird strain of music, floated into the room from the court. Anna d'Arquista hurried to the window and saw Taki, the Indian, sitting on a low stone bench with the flute at his lips.

"Do you hear? Do you hear?" asked Lucia in great excitement.

"It is beautifully played . . . yes."

"But the words . . . the words."

"What are they?"

"It is an old Scotch ballad. Listen!"

She began to sing:

> Ye highlands and ye lowlands,
> Oh, where hae ye been?
> They hae slain the Earl of Murray
> And they laid him on the green.
> Now wae be to ye, Huntly,
> And wherefore did ye sae?
> I bade ye bring him wi' you
> And forbade ye him to slay!

There the music of the flute stopped.

"It is his message! It is his message!" breathed the girl.

"Lucia, what under heaven do you mean? What message in the playing of a flute?"

"But the words of the old song, Aunt Anna! Don't you see? He puts himself in my hands!"

"Lucia, go instantly to Señor Torreño!"

"Not for a million pesos!"

"Then I . . ."

"Aunt Anna, if you betray him, I shall never forgive you. Never!"

VII

In the meantime, as the dusk settled, there began through the house a great bustle. Servants ran here and there. Beyond the court, men were seen putting up tents. Everywhere were voices of command and scurrying feet. It would have been a simple thing for Lucia to call her maids and ask her question of them. But she preferred to go to the window and speak through it to the Indian. He rose and came before her instantly.

"Someone has come, Taki. Run and learn who it is."

"It is the Señor Hernandez Guadalmo. He has come to take shelter here with my master."

"How could you know all of this, Taki, without leaving this little court?"

"No man other than Señor Guadalmo would travel with so great a train. Besides, I have heard them speak his name as they ran about."

"He is some great man, then, traveling with such a train?"

"He is a friend of the governor. He has monopolies. He is very rich."

"Does he not carry his own tents then?"

"Those are his tents they are putting up yonder. But Señor Guadalmo prefers to sleep behind strong walls, señorita."

"Why is that? Is he afraid of the night air?"

Taki smiled a little, a very little—more with his eyes than with his lips.

"The night air is sometimes very bad. Men go to sleep strong and very well. They are dead when they waken."

"Taki! Is there some frightful plague here in California?"

"Yes, señorita."

"What are the symptoms of it?"

"The instant they are seen, the man is already dead."

"You speak of the men. Does it never touch the women?"

"Rarely, señorita."

"This is very strange. What are the symptoms, then?"

"They are different," said Taki. "Sometimes the man who was strong and well goes to sleep and is found in the morning with a great cut across his throat. Sometimes there is no outward mark, but his body is swollen . . ."

"Do you mean throat-cutting and poison, Taki?"

"But the symptom that is usually found," said Taki, without answering her less obliquely, "is the handle of a knife standing over the man's breast, with the blade fixed in his heart."

She frowned at him seriously. "It is a murderous country, then? Why?"

"The law is far away."

"And this Guadalmo is very much afraid?"

"Very, señorita."

"Is he a coward?"

"He is a famous fighter . . . a very brave man. In Spain his name was famous."

"Guadalmo, the duelist! Is it he?"

"It is, señorita."

"I have heard that he feared nothing . . . not even God, or the devil."

"There was a time when he did not. He would ride alone a thousand miles."

"What changed him?"

"There is one man who follows him. Five times he has tried to get the life of Señor Guadalmo. And five times he has nearly succeeded. Therefore, Señor Guadalmo has surrounded himself with great warriors. They would sooner get out their swords than take off their hats. They would rather fight than eat. These men protect him."

"Who is this man who follows Guadalmo?"

"No one can tell. It is a mystery. Some people say that it is the devil himself who has come for Señor Guadalmo, because no man would dare to face him."

"That is nonsense!"

"There are others who believe that it is merely the brother of a man Señor Guadalmo killed."

"Tell me of that."

"A hundred long marches to the East, señorita, there are many cities."

"The English colonies. I know."

"A trader came from them. He was called John Gidden. He had a ship which he commanded, and he traded here for hides. Señor Guadalmo and he dined together one day, and quarreled over some little thing. But when the wine had died in them, Señor Guadalmo sent for Gidden and told him he was sorry and asked him to come to his house. Señor Gidden came. In the night they quarreled again. They fought, and with swords. Señor Gidden was killed."

"If it was fair fight, Taki . . ."

"It was fair fight, señorita. This Señor Gidden was one who

lived by the sea. He had strong hands and a fearless heart. But the only weapons he knew were a cutlass and a pistol. A rapier was strange to him. However, he fought Señor Guadalmo, the great duelist, with a rapier. Therefore, being a fool, he was killed."

"That has an ugly sound, Taki."

"If he had not been a fool, he would have fought with a cutlass or with a saber."

"Perhaps he was not allowed?"

Taki made a gesture.

"As for that, I cannot tell. But he was killed . . . and afterward a letter came to Señor Guadalmo from the brother of this Señor Gidden, saying that he was coming to find Guadalmo and to kill him. And, after that, five times a masked man has set on Señor Guadalmo, as I have said, and five times Señor Guadalmo's life has been saved by a miracle. Therefore, he loves strong walls around him when he sleeps at night, and he has come this evening to beg a shelter from Señor Torreño."

"This is a strange story, Taki. However, I wish also to tell you that it has given me a thought. You are a fighting man, Taki."

"I, señorita? Among the Navajos I was a chief and a warrior. But the poor Indian is a child among the white men. His hands may be strong, but his wits are weak."

She chuckled. "However," she said, "since there is this plague in the land, I feel that I need a guard, and, while you are with me, you must be my protector, Taki."

"The señorita has commanded," said Taki, his eye as blank as ever. "I pray to the Great Spirit that my hand may be strong for her."

"You speak sadly, Taki."

"Ah," said Taki, "how can the guard of fighting men help us when there are other dangers which fighting men cannot face?"

"That sounds like a riddle. What dangers, Taki?"

"I have spoken too much," said Taki. "I am not the guard who can help the señorita."

"What guard should I have, then?"

"A father confessor," said the Indian calmly.

"A priest! And what would he do for me?"

"He would listen to the troubles which are in your heart, señorita!"

She had almost invited the blow, but when it came, it shocked her. She stiffened a little and drew back from the window.

"Your tongue," she said, "runs faster than your horse."

At that he made her a ceremonious bow. Certainly the lessons of the dancing master had not been entirely thrown away upon Taki. As for the girl, she did not pause to wonder over his grace, but she turned in anger to her Aunt Anna and saw, from her grave, sad face, that she had overheard everything.

"I shall go instantly to Señor Torreño," said the girl, "and tell him what I suspect of Taki."

Aunt Anna d'Arquista merely shook her head.

"I think you will not, Lucia," she said. "I pray God may rule us for the best."

She seemed so close to tears that Lucia dared not speak again, for the moment. She stormed into her room, and there she flung herself down on her bed. Her face was burning. And cold little pangs of shame shot through her heart.

She had thought that she controlled her tragedy so well that not a human being in the world could ever have guessed at it. But here was a wild Indian who had looked through her at a glance and, in a moment, had read all her secrets. She wanted to destroy him utterly. And yet, after a time, she found herself sitting up, musing and almost smiling.

"He is a clever rascal," said the girl to herself. "And if I were in a great need, he could help me."

She was called for the night meal after this, and met the guest, Guadalmo. He was a tall, wide-shouldered man of about forty, with a grim face and a gray head that might have been ten years older. His body was still young and supple—the body of the professional duelist. He bore traces of his encounters—a ragged scar in his right cheek and another which crossed one eye and kept it half closed so that he bore, continually, a quizzical, penetrating expression. He had donned his most magnificent clothes for this occasion. He wore, above all, old-fashioned lace cuffs and a great lace collar worth a fortune in skill and labor. It made an odd setting for his forbidding features.

He was a courtly man as well as a warrior, however. And he entertained the girl with talk of Paris and the French court, full of little cuts and thrusts of gossip. He was one of those who can speak with an easy familiarity of the great men of the world and seem to bring their presences into the room. Don Carlos listened to him, agape with delight.

"Tomorrow," said Don Carlos, "I shall beg five minutes of your time to teach me some clever thrust. I have been shamed by an Indian, with the foils. I must have some revenge on him."

Guadalmo raised his brows. "An Indian," he said, "who fences?"

"The skill of a fiend incarnate," said Torreño, breaking in. "I should give a great deal to see you cross blades with him, señor."

Señor Guadalmo smiled.

"For Indians," he said, "I keep a whip . . . and bullets. I advise you, my dear friends, to do the same."

Here a door behind Guadalmo swung silently open, but he knew it by the soft sighing of the draft, and leaped violently to his feet, setting all the dishes on the table in a great jangle. He had a pistol in his hand as he whirled, but he saw behind him only an empty threshold, dimly lighted.

"Señor! Señor!" cried the host. "One would think that you feared the Masked Rider even in the midst of my household!"

"Set a man to watch the door," requested Guadalmo, reseating himself, but still with a pale face. "I have a profound respect for your household and your management of it, Señor Torreño. But when one has to do with the devil . . . one needs caution . . . caution . . . and, again, caution!"

The effect of that fright was still ghastly in his face, but with an inward struggle, he forced a smile to his lips again.

He took up a glass of white wine in which the imaged light of a candle flame was trembling. The girl noted that the tremor was not in the flame of the candle, but in the hand of Guadalmo. She observed and she wondered. And when a breath of air through the open window set the draperies behind her shivering and whispering, she trembled in turn, as though the ghost of the Masked Rider were behind her chair!

VIII

Who is the Masked Rider? It was the commanding question in the mind of the girl when she went out into the
patio beneath the stars with the others. From the little white
tent city around the main house, all the retainers of Don
Francisco were waxing merry and raising songs from time to
time, and, at the end of each day's work, the followers of the
worthy don received due portions of that colorless brandy
which the Mexican Indian loves and which burns the brain
of the white man like a blue flame. But even their singing
was subdued, for Don Francisco hated all loud noise, except
that of his own strong voice.

Obviously no questions about the Masked Rider could be
asked while Señor Guadalmo was himself present, but after an
uneasy moment, he bade the rest goodnight and withdrew to
his appointed quarters for sleep—or so he said. But during an
interval which followed, they could hear the stir of men.

"Guadalmo is filling the house with his guards," said
Torreño. "Look! Even under his window!"

They saw two stalwarts, each with sword and carbine, take

post beneath the windows of Guadalmo's room. There they remained, huge, black specters.

"I have an idea," said the girl. "The Masked Rider is one of Señor Guadalmo's men with a grudge against him."

Torreño chuckled in the bottom of his thick throat.

"My dear," he said, "that is child's talk. You do not know Guadalmo and his men. He has picked up the neatest set of murderers that ever wore sword and pistol since the beginning of time. There is not a one of them that does not owe his escape from the gallows to his master. They live by him . . . They would be hung except for him and his influence with the governor. They know it, and they would fight for him as for themselves. He is their safety; he is their charm against death. Those two men yonder . . . I can tell the one by the feather in his hat, the other by the limp in his walk. The tall man used to cut throats in Naples . . . Guadalmo smuggled him aboard his ship and made off with him. The other was a soldier in the Low Countries, a gambler who made up for his losses on the highway. He fled to Guadalmo also. So they are here. They will watch over him more tenderly than they will watch over their own souls!"

"But this Masked Rider, has he never appeared except to Señor Guadalmo?"

"Some dozen times," said Don Carlos. "He knows, it appears, whenever some solitary traveler sets out with a large sum of money. Then the Masked Rider appears. Usually he sweeps up from behind on a horse swifter than the wind, it is said. The animal is sheathed in a light caparison of dark silk. There is a hood of thin dark silk covering the rider, too. That is how he gets his name. He stops his man, takes his purse, and is gone. Sometimes they were brave and resisted, at the first. A bullet in the leg or through the shoulder always ended the fight. The Masked Rider does not kill. He does not have to. He can see in the dark, it seems, and he shoots with such a nice aim that he could kill a bat on the wing at midnight!"

That was all the explanation she received concerning the Masked Rider. After his first few captures, the mere terror of his presence had proved enough to paralyze all resistance. Men were benumbed with fear when he approached.

At last Lucia stood up to go to her room, and, as she turned, it seemed to her that there was a movement in the far corner of the patio.

"In the name of heaven, Señor Torreño," she breathed.

The shadow stirred. A man stood upright.

"Carlos . . . fool . . . your pistol!" growled out Torreño.

"It is I . . . Taki," said the shadow.

"Tie the red-face to a post and have him whipped!" commanded Torreño. "Have you turned into a spy, Taki?"

"It is the command of the señorita," said the Indian. "I am to stay close to her to protect her in case of harm."

"Seven thousand devils!" thundered the other. "Am I not guard enough for her, and in my own house? Lucia, what madness is this?"

"Only, Señor Torreño," she said, "because he was given to me, and I did not know what other work to give him."

"Well," said Torreño, "you must not be afraid of the ghosts you make with your own hands. But for half of a second, I looked at him and thought . . . the Masked Rider!"

"Is the Masked Rider so large a man?"

"Larger, it is said. A very giant! A span taller than this Taki of yours. Goodnight!"

Don Carlos went with her to the door of her room. Taki was three paces to the rear.

"Dear Lucia," he said, as they paused there, "now that you

have seen my father and his country, do you think that you can be happy among us and our rude people?"

She looked up to him with a little twisted smile. "Ah, Carlos," she said, "I should be afraid to say no to the son of Don Francisco." And she hurried on into the room with Anna d'Arquista.

Don Carlos turned to speak to Taki, but that man of the silent foot had already disappeared.

There was no definite quarters assigned to the Indian. He was left to shift for himself, and the place he had chosen was in a nook behind a hedge. There, from a blanket roll, he provided himself with what he wanted, which was chiefly a mask of dark silk, fitting closely over his face, a pistol, and a rapier. Provided with these, he made his way back toward the house, moving swiftly but with caution and going, wherever possible, in the gloom beneath the trees, for the moon was up, now, and the open places were silvered with faint light. He came to the wall of the big, squat house and moved around it until a form loomed in front of him.

A short-barreled musket was instantly thrust against his breast. Yet the voice of the guard was muffled, lest he needlessly disturb the slumber of his master.

"Who is this?" he asked.

"I am the new man."

"I know of no new man."

The footfalls of another sentinel, who kept guard around the corner of the wall, paused at the end of his beat. In a moment he would be back and in view of them.

Taki drew in his breath and tensed his muscles. "I have ridden all afternoon up from the harbor," he said.

"Ah?"

"You are Giovanni?"

"Yes."

"I have brought you a message."

"From whom?"

"Naples."

"Diablo!" breathed the other. "Are you from Naples?"

And he lowered the muzzle of his gun a trifle. In that instant Taki struck the other with bone-crushing force on the base of the jaw, and he slumped gently forward on his face. Taki stepped over him.

"Giovanni?" he heard the other guard murmur as he approached the corner of the wall.

And then the second man turned the corner and came full against Taki. He had no time to cry out. The left hand of the Indian, like a steel-clawed panther's foot, was fixed instantly on his throat. And as his breath stopped, he snatched a knife from his belt. But Taki struck with the hilt of his rapier, and the guard turned limp in his grip.

After that, in a single minute of swift work, as one familiar with such things, he gagged them with their own garments and bound them back to back. Then he flattened himself against the wall and looked around him.

All was quiet in the house; only from the distance came an amiable, musical hum of voices from the tents; a reassuring sound of men at peace with one another and with the world. And Taki's teeth glinted white as he smiled at the moon. Then he turned, adjusted the silken mask, laid a hand on the sill of the open window, and drew himself softly into the room.

Señor Don Hernandez Guadalmo slept but lightly, and even that silken smooth entrance of the Indian's had roused him. Now, as Taki turned from the window, he faced Guadalmo, who was sitting bolt upright in his bed, but so paralyzed with nightmare horror that he could not move his hand. Before he recovered, Taki had clapped a pistol to his head.

"Don Hernandez, son of a dog," he said, "for the sixth time, we have met."

"God receive my soul," murmured the wretched man.

"The devil will receive it," said the other. "But not from this room. You must step out with me, señor."

"If you have murder to do, do it here. But first, let me see your face."

"Before you die, you shall see it, I promise. And if I fail, you may use your discretion upon me. Here, Señor Guadalmo, is your favorite sword. I make free to borrow it. Now, step before me through that window. If you cry out, if you attempt to run, I send a bullet through your back . . . or an ounce of lead to mingle with your brains, my friend."

"What reward is there in the end?"

"A chance to fight with me fairly, point to point, sword to sword, and die like a murderer, as you deserve, but also like a gentleman."

Guadalmo fairly trembled with joy. "Is it true?"

"On the honor of one whose faith has never been broken."

"I go as to a feast," said the duelist. He paused only to draw on a few garments. Then he slipped through the window before Taki and was rejoined by him on the ground.

"The guards?" he queried in a whisper.

Taki pointed to a tangled heap of shadow at the corner of the wall. "They will not notice you are going, señor."

"You have confederates who have done this?"

"Confederates? Yes, my two hands. Walk straight ahead, señor. I shall remain just half a pace behind you."

"My friend, the Masked Rider," said Hernandez Guadalmo, "this promises to be a notable and happy night."

And he walked straight forward down the slope and into the hollow beneath.

IX

"Here," said the Indian, "we will be very comfortable."

Guadalmo paused. He found himself in a little level-bottomed clearing surrounded by the squat forms of oak trees, each with a dim, black pattern printed beneath them on the brown grass.

The moon was bright. A cool sea wind stirred across the hollow and brought to it the indescribable freshness of salt water. And from the highlands came the additional scent of the evergreens.

Guadalmo cast off the light cloak from his shoulders.

"I am ready, señor," he said.

"Your sword," replied the other, and presented it to him by tossing it lightly through the air. Guadalmo caught it with considerable dexterity and made the blade whistle in the air.

"Now God be praised. Señor, the Masked Rider," he said, "I see that I have to do with a gentleman and not with a cutthroat."

"Be assured, friend," said the Indian dryly, "that if I were a throat cutter, yours would have been slashed at our first meeting. This is to be a fair fight with equal weapons."

"However, you still carry a pistol at your belt."

The Indian tossed that weapon behind him and into the shrubbery.

"We are now even forces."

There was a ring of joy in the throat of Guadalmo.

"Fool," he said, "you are no better than a dead man. If you dare to stand up to me for ten breaths, I promise you a swift road to heaven. But as for equal forces . . . if I am hard-pressed, I have only to shout, and a dozen men will come for me."

Taki started, then shook his head as though to reassure himself.

"I have thought of that, of course," he said calmly, "but I think that I know you too well. For you had rather die, Guadalmo, than have men know that you cried out for help against a single man."

"Come, come!" exclaimed the Spaniard. "The time flies. If the bound guards are found and I am missed, there will be a noise at once."

"That is true. Señor, on guard!"

Their blades whipped up in a formal salute. Continuing the same motion, Guadalmo passed on into a murderous lunge. Only a backward stroke saved Taki from that treacherous move.

"Ah, murderer," he breathed. "This is your beginning."

"Save your breath for your work. You shall have plenty of it," said Guadalmo, and attacked instantly.

He came in with the reckless abandon of one accustomed to looking upon his narrow rapier as a secure wall of steel against his enemy's point. And the blade of Taki met his with a continual, harsh clattering. Neither would give back. They pressed on to half sword length.

"Ha!" cried the Spaniard through his teeth, and delivered

an upward thrust at the throat against which there seemed no possible ward.

But Taki found one. With his bare hand, he knocked aside the darting weapon. He stepped in with the same movement and crushed Guadalmo against his breast. The hug of the bear could not have been more paralyzing.

"I am a dead man! God receive me!" gasped out Guadalmo as the point of the shortened sword appeared at his throat.

"With that stroke, señor," said Taki, "you killed Antonio Cadoral in Padua. Tonight, it has failed you. What else have you left?"

He cast the helpless man away.

"Breathe again, Guadalmo," he said. "Now, señor, your utmost skill."

"Devil!" groaned Guadalmo. "You have only a minute to live!"

And he attacked not recklessly but with the utmost deadliness of finesse, working as though a picture were being drawn by the point of his weapon. It became a play of double lightning, the two blades flashing in the glow of the moonlight.

But the minute passed and Taki still lived, and without giving ground. He began to talk again as they worked, as one who held his task lightly.

"Señor Guadalmo, there is a grove near Toledo where a gallant gentleman, Juan Jaratta, met you without seconds. You killed him with foul play . . . a sudden thrust when, by mutual agreement, you had lowered your swords to take a breath."

"It is false!" snarled out Guadalmo. "Besides, there was no human eye near to take note of such a thing."

"I, however, was nearby, and watched."

"You are the devil, then!"

"As you please. But beware, Guadalmo. For the sake of Jaratta, I am about to touch you over the heart!"

"I defy you!"

The rapier in the hand of Taki darted out as the humming-bird darts toward the deep mouth of a flower—and as the hummingbird stops dead in mid-flight and then shoots forward again, a mere flash of rainbow color and sheen, so the blade of Taki paused and drove beneath the parry of Guadalmo, and the keen point pricked him on the breast.

"Damnation!" gasped out Guadalmo, and quickly leaped backward with all his power.

He began to perspire with the weakness not of exhaustion, but of despair and fear.

"We have only begun," said Taki. "There was in Nice, on a time, a young gentleman from the American colonies of England. He had loaned you money, Guadalmo, and when your time came to repay it, you found a quarrel with him and met him outside the city on a broad green lawn. There were great flowers planted around the lawn. As the dawn grew clear, you could see their colors . . . golden-yellow, bronze, and deepest scarlet. Do you remember?"

"If I remember, you shall soon forget. So!"

"A good thrust," said Taki, putting the stroke aside with a flick of his own blade. "And a favorite in Bologna. With it, in fact, you killed the poor gentleman. And, for his sake, another touch above the heart . . ."

Who can escape the leap of the lightning? Señor Guadalmo was tense with dreadful anxiety, and yet he could not avoid the sudden flash of Taki's sword. And again there was a beesting in the flesh above his heart. He felt a little warm trickle of blood run down inside his shirt—warm blood over a body that had turned to ice.

He gave ground. He looked wildly up the slope above the trees, where the roofs of the house of Torreño were faintly visible. There was succor, in ample scope, so near, so near! He thought of turning and fleeing toward it, but as he watched the tigerish smoothness of the advance of Taki, he knew that he would be overtaken in a single leap. There was no escape that way. He thought of crying out—but before the sound had left his lips, the inescapable mischief which played so brightly in the hand of the tall man would be buried in his heart. And the cold perspiration streamed down the face of Guadalmo. His body was dank with it.

"There are still others," said Taki. "You have covered your way with killings, damnable murders made legal. You have picked quarrels with young men who had scarcely left their fencing masters after a month of practice. But above all, there was one man who had never held a straight sword in his life. He was an honest sailor, Guadalmo. An honest man, do you hear me? A breath of his was worth more than your eternal soul. He was a kind, bluff man. All who knew him, loved him. He had behind him a young wife and two small children. Ah, Guadalmo, my friend, what a devil it would have taken to murder that honorable man. And yet there was such a demon in the world. There was such a murder done. All honorable! He was challenged and met with rapiers. He was forced to fight, he thought, to defend his honor. His honor against a rat, a snake, a wolf! Think of it, Señor Guadalmo. Can you conceive it?"

"Are you done?" snarled out Guadalmo, perceiving that the end was near. "Are you done whining? Yes, I killed him. And you are his brother? Hear me, friend. When the steel went through him, he screamed like a woman!"

Taki groaned. "He screamed with agony of sorrow, because he thought of his wife and his family . . . with bewilderment that such a tiny needle of a weapon should have taken his life . . . but never with pain or with fear. For he was a lion, Señor Guadalmo. And it is for his sake that I am about to touch you for the third time, and this time, you are to die! Think of him, and how he lay in your patio, panting and gasping. He had messages which he begged you to send to his wife. He would forgive you, pray for you, if you would send them. Did you send them, Guadalmo? Did you send them? A word, only, to his widow or his orphans?"

"Bah!" gasped out the Spaniard, and lunged with all his force.

It was like attacking a will-o'-the-wisp. He closed again with a shout of despair. Then a limber hand of steel closed around his sword. He felt a wrench that twisted his wrist far to one side. Out of his wet fingers the sword was drawn, and flipped high into the air, spinning over and over, brilliant against the moon, in its fall. And Guadalmo followed it with eyes of horror and of bewilderment.

He looked down at the leveled blade of his opponent. And then, from the rear of the clearing, a pistol spoke, a bullet hummed past and thudded heavily against the body of an oak tree, and into the open ran three men. There was a wild cry of rage from Taki. He leaped at Guadalmo with a final lunge, but the latter fell groveling upon the ground and missed death by a fraction of a second. Over him leaped Taki—no time for a second stroke.

Another bound brought him among the shadows of the trees—and he was gone, with a final volley whirring about him.

And, in the meantime, it seemed that a hundred voices had suddenly begun to shout at the same time, before him and behind him.

There was no pursuit on the part of the valiants, however. They did not care to follow the tiger into his lair among the crowded trees; they preferred to make a close guard around

Guadalmo and shout for help. So Taki paused to drop the rapier into a shallow bed of leaves. He snatched the mask from his face.

Just before him a body of six men broke in among the trees.

"Who is there?" they shouted to him.

"Taki," he said. And he joined in the hunt.

X

It was a matter not to be mentioned in the presence of Señor Torreño. It was well enough if some rascally brigand dared to hold up passersby upon the great highway. But when they ventured into his very presence and there committed their villainies, it was high time that an end were put to these proceedings. Señor Torreño ordered his entire household to mount. He left at the house a mere guard of half a dozen men. With the rest, he scoured the country. And, conspicuous among the foremost riders was Taki, the Navajo, who distinguished himself by being the only man of the party who thought he saw a fugitive vanishing among the hills. However, they could not trace the vision of Taki, and therefore they eventually turned back to the house, gloomy and disgruntled. The lips of Torreño flowed curses faster than a well gives forth water. He damned the entire world in general and the Masked Rider in particular. He began again with the Masked Rider and went backward, damning the entire world. He would burn the entire region of California to a crisp, but in the end he would have this reckless manhunter who ventured upon his kill in the very lair of the Torreño himself!

The story Guadalmo told Torreño was simple and clear. He had been wakened from sleep by having a cord thrown around his body. Therefore, he awakened helpless. He was forced to dress in haste and climb down through the window, and so was taken to the hollow where he was eventually found. There he was, about to be murdered, but he had managed to excite the pride of the Masked Rider sufficiently to make the outlaw begin a single-handed duel in the course of which he was about to spit the Masked Rider like a chicken, and so put an end to that sinister public plague, when they were broken in upon by fools who thought they were running to the rescue. It made no difference that the rescuers, according to what their eyes had told them, vowed that they did not notice any sword in the hand of Guadalmo. They were not believed to have seen what was before them. For, though it was conceivable that the great Guadalmo might be conquered in fight, it was notably ridiculous to conceive that he had been so overmastered that he was actually disarmed!

Señor Guadalmo, however, made light of the whole matter when they sat together to break their fast in the morning, after the futile manhunt had ended.

"Now that I have seen this ghost face to face, and noted the color of his eyes," said Guadalmo, "I assure you that there will soon be an end to him. Oh, fool, fool, fool that I was!"

He struck his palm across his forehead and sighed.

"What is wrong, Guadalmo?" asked his host.

"When I think that I might have put this monster out of the world with a mere touch . . . and that I allowed him to live! Alas, Torreño, I am covered with shame and with fury."

"Tell us, Guadalmo."

"No, no! It sickens me to think of it! Fool, fool that I was!"

"We must hear it, señor."

"It was in this manner. We had closed. We were at hardly

more than half sword distance. I threw him off balance with a strong parry and at the same instant I closed on him and took him by the throat. The dog lost heart at once. He dropped his sword and fell on his knees and babbled out a prayer for mercy. Mercy has ever been my besetting sin. I could not kill that wild beast even when I had him in that position."

Lady Anna d'Arquista fairly trembled with admiration. To think that at the same table with her sat a man who had been able to crush the famous Masked Rider to his knees was enough to make her shudder. She said to her niece: "Did you ever see such a gallant and noble gentleman, Lucia?"

Lucia wasn't always graceful in her manners. Now she grunted as a man might have done, and a very rough man at that.

"He has a sick look," she said.

"Guadalmo?"

"He has had troubles enough to last him out the month," said the girl, nodding her head sagely.

"Of course, to be wakened by that fiend . . ."

"A poor, weak devil!" scoffed the girl. "Our great Guadalmo takes him by the throat and makes the devil beg!"

"You do not believe?"

"Of course I believe," said Lucia, yawning a little. "I believe anything that is amusing. There is little enough, at that."

She could not be moved from this position. Guadalmo finished his recital in the midst of a silence which was a greater tribute than applause. He promised, however, that when he had a little spare time on his hands, he would hunt down this wretched road-haunter, this Masked Rider, and cut him to shreds the very next time they encountered each other.

Here Lucia spoke aloud: "The next time, señor," she said, "will surely be the last. It will be the seventh. And that number is surely fatal, is it not?"

To the surprise of everyone, Señor Guadalmo turned white, and his face was glistening with perspiration.

"I pray heaven, señorita," he said in a shaken voice, "that you are not a prophet."

"Ah, ah!" cried Lucia. "I mean, of course, that the meeting will be fatal for him . . . for the Masked Rider!"

It was too late to give the thought that turn in the mind of Guadalmo. He seemed stricken. He sat bowed in his chair, his head in his hand.

He said over and over: "There is a sort of fate in it, is there not? I meet him again and again . . . I alone. Six times he has encountered me . . . six times the breath of the devil has fanned my cheek. But all this is only a warning. The seventh time the devil will gather me in!"

He removed himself from the table presently and went from the room. All remained in an uneasy silence for a moment behind him.

At length Torreño himself murmured: "Who would have believed this of the great Guadalmo?"

His steward came in at that moment. He was full of excitement. He reported that, in a shallow bed of leaves in the forest, not far from the very spot where Señor Guadalmo had been found in close fight with the marauder, one of the peons had stumbled into a hidden sword and got a shrewd cut in the leg for his discovery. It was given to the steward, who instantly gave it, of course, to the master of the house. Could it be, by any chance, the weapon of the Masked Rider, which had fallen from his hand? Torreño took the rapier and held it at arm's length.

"That is a rapier worthy of a gentleman, not a brigand," he said. "I'll swear that the Masked Rider would rather have parted with so much flesh nearest his heart than to have lost this weapon. At least, we have one of the feathers of the crow, which is more than all the other hunters for him can say. But what if he comes back for it?"

Here there followed an impressive little silence, and into it ran the sound of a far-off flute:

> Ye highlands and ye lowlands,
> Oh, where hae ye been?
> They hae slain the Earl of Murray
> And hae laid him on the green.
> Now wae be to thee, Huntly,
> And wherefore did ye sae?
> I bade ye bring him wi' you
> And forbade ye him to slay.

Then Señor Torreño stood up. He sent for Guadalmo. He sent for half a dozen other of his most trusted men—and then changed his mind and took with him the same number of Guadalmo's practiced fighters.

"This hand-to-hand fighting and this dueling," he said, "is all very well. But I prefer a net which is sure of catching the bird."

The wounded servant limped along to show them the way; it was a perfect place. Low shrubbery enclosed a little hollow, and in that pool of leaves, stirred by only the strongest winds, the rapier had been found. Guadalmo and the rest instantly took cover among the shrubs. In the meantime, orders were sent back for the rest of the train to be busy preparing the coach and packing up for the journey.

If the Masked Rider were nearby, watching, he might venture down even now to secure his lost weapon!

But nothing came near them except the sound of the flute of Taki, the Navajo, as he wandered casually among the trees.

He appeared, presently, from among them. He came to the pool of the dead leaves and scuffed through it. He turned, still with the flute at his lips, and went shuffling through the leaves again.

Then he stopped, lowered the flute, and frowned. Presently he leaned over and slipped his hand among the leaves. It seemed, indeed, as though he were searching for something. And what he wanted was not there! He dropped to his knees, then, and, pocketing the flute, he was busy with both hands.

Suddenly, the voice of Guadalmo rang loudly as he started up.

"Take him, my friends! This is the man we want!"

They started out of the shrubbery like six bloodhounds. Instantly, they closed around the tall form of the Indian. He was still a head above the tallest man. He made no resistance. He merely looked about him in a bewildered fashion as they laid hands upon him. Torreño came storming from his place. The Masked Rider was a man of wit and invention, a dashing, clever fellow. This was no more than a red Indian and could not be the man.

"He has come here to hunt . . . for what?" asked Guadalmo. "For his lost sword, of course. Besides, I have heard his voice . . . I have seen his height and his form. It is the man, Torreño. My life on it! Another thing . . . give me hot water and a little scrubbing, and you will see some of the red come from that skin. None but a white man could handle a sword as he handles his. I'll go a step farther, my friends. I'll give him a name . . . which is Gidden!"

So much surety turned the scales at once.

"Bring him instantly to the house," said Torreño. "We'll have a try with water at his hide."

"There is no need, señor," said the prisoner calmly. "I freely confess that I am Richard Gidden!"

Señor Guadalmo began to laugh. The lines of trouble

disappeared from his face. Years of age seemed to have been stripped from him.

"Taki," he said, "would have given the hounds a run, but Richard Gidden will be found worthy of hanging. Is it not so, Torreño?"

XI

To this question, the master of those lands did not immediately return an answer. He looked about him with a vacant eye of thought over the brown hills and the dark patches of oak groves here and there, studded with a scattering of cattle. Then he turned to Guadalmo.

"This man is worthy of death," he said at length. "That is clear. He confesses it himself. Now, my friend, when I see a white man, I am ready to give him a white man's death. But when I see a redskin, an Indian's death is a better thing for him. His skin is red. He calls himself Richard Gidden. It is an odd name. He is known to me only as Taki. And as Taki I swear he shall die."

"And how?" asked Guadalmo, falling in readily enough with the viewpoint of the other. "For my part, I say, tie his hands behind his back and send a few ounce bullets through his head. That will make an end of him. However, there may be better ways. What way, Señor Torreño?"

"The dogs!" said Torreño. "I have traveled without them for this time only. But you have them with you constantly. The dogs, Guadalmo, and a fifty-pace start for him!"

"Señor Guadalmo," broke in Richard Gidden, "your life has been in my hands, and I have spared it. Remember!"

"My life in your hands?" snarled out the Spaniard. "You lie, you rat! Besides, my pack need a blooding. They have grown dull on the trail. Yes, the dogs, Torreño, the dogs! An Indian's death for a redskin."

And the first man to echo that cry among the followers of Señor Guadalmo was none other than Giovanni of Naples, with a bruised patch at the base of his jaw and a fury of rage in his heart. It was taken up; it swept to the house; it reached the ears even of the lady, Lucia. She could not understand, at first, but when she did, she went straight to Don Carlos. He was about to hurry to the manhunt, with gaiety in his face.

"Carlos," she said with a sort of stern eagerness, "if you wish my love and my respect, stop this hideous thing. He is a man, Carlos, not a beast. And they tell me he is a white man. God in heaven knows that I guessed that before I had heard him speak three words. For the sake of your soul . . . for my sake, Carlos, stop this hunt! And if . . ."

Her voice was broken short by a loud clamor of deep-voiced hounds. She beckoned him away and turned to the house with her head bowed, her hands pressed over her ears. Don Carlos left her like a frightened boy who has seen a mystery. It had never occurred to him that it was wrong to hunt Indians with dogs. He had done it. His father had enjoyed that same wild sport. What there was in it of sin he could not see. And for the fact that the man was white, it was obvious that since he had chosen the disguise of a redskin, an Indian's death was only ironically proper to him. And yet, seeing the horror in the face of the girl, he comprehended dimly that there was both a crime and a sin here. Most of all, he was afraid of her. He would have faced anything rather than incur her displeasure. He would have faced his very father. And, a moment later, he did so.

The hounds were out, and Torreño was discussing their merits rather than the merits of the work which was before them. The admirable Señor Guadalmo had in person brought this pack from Germany. The base of their blood was the boarhound. But having been trained by the skillful hand of Guadalmo, they were soon accustomed to course far nobler game. Huge of shoulder and quarter, with great, square, muzzled heads and brows wrinkled with lionlike sagacity and fierceness, they possessed, in addition, long limbs and the tucked-up bellies of greyhounds which were token of their speed. There were a dozen in the original pack. Seven remained, but they were like seven tigers in ferocity and cunning. Already they sensed work to their liking, and raged on the leashes. Two servants held each dog—and each dog was worth the price of two peons! The entire household was gathered to watch the chase. It was now that Don Carlos encountered his father.

"Señor," he said, "for the grace of heaven, do not hunt this man with the dogs."

His father turned slowly upon him. He had been touched to the very core of the heart with rage by the invasion of his house the night before. Now he saw some chance to let loose the gathering thunder of his anger.

"The grace of heaven? The grace of heaven?" he echoed. "What do you know of the grace of heaven, boy?"

Don Carlos was stricken. He retreated a pace. His voice trembled a little as he added: "It is not I who ask, Father," he said. "It is Lucia."

"It is Lucia!" mocked Torreño, putting a semi-awe into his own tones. "It is the peerless lady, Lucia. Now, boy, hear me and understand me. I have paid a price for that girl. And may my soul roast if the price was not high. There is one way she may make me a return for my money . . . and that is to be an obedient daughter. But as for what she wishes . . . damnation, Carlos, am I to be ruled by the whims of a girl and a fool? Am I to be ruled? I?"

His voice had raised at the end.

Don Carlos was fairly quaking with fear.

Yet still he remembered the face of Lucia and so he persisted for a moment.

"Alas, sir," he said. "If you had seen her as I saw her, when she begged me to . . ."

"Begged?" said Torreño, breaking strongly in. "That is good! Teach her to beg. She is too apt to demand. As for this business, she knows nothing about it. A woman's gentleness would fill this land with red devils in a month. It is one of my servants, Carlos, who dared to enter my house and raised a hand against a guest of Francisco Torreño! I will see him torn to shreds! Do you hear me?"

"I hear you," said Don Carlos submissively.

"As for the girl, your wife to be," continued Torreño, a little appeased by the frightened face of his son, "she may weep today, frown tomorrow, and sulk the next day. Then give her a ring . . . a horse . . . or some other trinket. And she will forget. Here is time to learn a great thing in the management of women, my lad. Let them feel the whip now and then . . . The whip, Carlos!"

He rubbed his hands together and laughed loudly.

"Now, friends!" he called to the others. "Is all prepared? Look to the cinches of my saddle, Juan. Mind his heels, fool! Señor Guadalmo, this will be sport!"

"Unless he runs away from the dogs," said Guadalmo with a discontented face. "The surest way is a bullet through the head. Let the dogs have him afterward, if you choose!"

He added in thunder: "Bring out Taki! Bring him out! Place him here!"

Fifty not overlong strides Torreño advanced before the leashed pack, and marked the spot by driving his heel into the ground. To that place they led out Richard Gidden, half-naked. There was no doubt about the true color of his skin now. All his body had been dyed copper, but only about the face and hands had the stain been carefully renewed. The rest of him was many a shade lighter, and across his shoulders the white seemed fairly shining through.

He came forth with a firm step. He regarded the beasts who were to hunt him. He watched the mounting of the riders. Then he turned his glance before him, as though selecting the best course for his race. He was rather like an athlete contending for a great prize than one about to struggle hopelessly for life.

"Cast him loose!" commanded Torreño. "Stand fast, Taki, until you hear the word. Stand fast, or we send a dozen bullets through you. Now, lads, with the dogs . . ."

The guards, who had surrounded the prisoner, now gave back in haste to open a channel through which the dogs might run at their prey. But by this time, they were in a frenzy of eagerness. They reared to a man's height as they strained at the leashes.

"Unleash!" cried Torreño. "Halloo! Away!"

A horn blew; the dogs leaped off, giving tongue, and Richard Gidden whirled to flee. But, as he whirled, he whistled once, a long, shrill note that cut through the air like the scream of a bagpipe. Then he fled down the slope toward the nearest hollow.

For fifty yards, with the fear of death winging his feet, he gained on the flying dogs, for the boarhound, after all, is a stout but clumsy runner. For a hundred yards, he held them even. Then they began to gain steadily and surely. They crossed the hollow. They sped up the slope beyond, with the hillside giving back their deep voices in thunder. They topped the first hill and lunged down into the gentle valley beyond. And now they were straining forward closer and closer to his heels. The leaders began to slaver. The note of the baying rose sharper and shorter as toward the kill. And the horsemen who swept at an easy canter in the rear shouted encouragement. Torreño was strangled with laughter; Señor Guadalmo, like a madman in his joy, yelled to the hounds and brandished his fist above his head.

By the time they reached the next hollow, they would pull down the fugitive, beyond doubt. The morning sun shone on Gidden's limbs, burnished with perspiration; his body swayed, now, with the agony of his labor, and his head was flagging back with exhaustion.

And then a red flash left the thicket to the left, and a red bay stallion flaunted across the open straight at the fugitive.

It was Guadalmo who first understood the meaning of the thing.

"Torreño!" he screamed. "Look! Look! His horse! Once on the back of that red devil, he is gone like the wind! Ride down the hounds. Get to him! Pistols and swords, my friends, if you love me! If he escapes today, we are but murdered men tomorrow!"

They heard him with a shout of rage, gave their horses the spur, and instantly they were among the pack and rushing fast upon the runner. But though they rode hard and recklessly down that slope like true cavaliers, their speed was nothing compared with the unburdened stallion. He came like a loose lightning flash, down the slope and into the hollow. Straight beside Gidden he rushed, and swerving there, with hardly abated gallop, they saw the fugitive fling himself at the bay, grapple the mane with one hand, take a long, winged leap as he was jerked forward by the running horse, and then rebound upward to his back.

But he was not yet free. The pursuit came hot behind him, and now their guns were out. But heavy horse pistols fired from the backs of running horses strike a target by chance rather than by skill. A dozen bullets combed the air about him as he lay flat on the back of the horse. But he guided the stallion by the touch of his hand to the left. Twenty paces before the pursuit, he reached the next grove of oaks. And the voice of Guadalmo was a moan of desperation.

Through the open grove they pushed, bringing blood with every stroke of their spurs. The pack of boarhounds strained far, far to the rear now, setting up what seemed a foolish clamor. As well might they try to catch the wind as to overtake this fugitive. He was work for their masters. Too much work, indeed, even for them. For when they gained the open again, the red bay was racing over the next hilltop, and when they reached the next hilltop, he was entering a broken copse of oak in the hollow.

For another ten minutes, they labored with curses and whip and spurs, but at the end of that time, Richard Gidden had vanished from among the hills! The chase halted. All were silent. Torreño's brow was black as a thundercloud. The lips of Guadalmo were twitching in a passion which he dared not release in words, for fear lest words alone would not suffice him. But the eye which he turned upon Torreño was the very soul of eloquence.

So they came back toward the house. The dogs followed on through the hills unregarded. Later, servants would pursue them a weary distance and bring them in once more. But they would bring no consolation to Torreño or to Guadalmo. Those captains rode with faces averted from one another and so regained their quarters. And the view of them as they came in with failure printed on their brows brought joy to one person only—and that was the Señorita Lucia. Anna d'Arquista had come running to her and found her in prayer at the foot of the altar in her little private chapel—passionate prayer, with her face pressed against the cold stone. She rose and ran to the window, and, looking out, she cried: "God has heard me! God has heard me!"

XII

The son, Señor Don Carlos Torreño, had enjoyed the race after Taki—or Richard Gidden, to give him his true name—as much as any man. But when the red stallion appeared and swept the fugitive away to safety, he was the dreariest of all the party who turned back toward the house—with the single exception of Señor Guadalmo. The duelist was thinking of death; Don Carlos was thinking of his lady. It would have been hard to say which of the two had the colder heart.

But, in the meantime, there was the bustle of starting on that day's journey, and during that time he was able to avoid the eye of Lucia. And when the carriage was lumbering along the road, at last, he was spared a face-to-face encounter with her again. For Hernandez Guadalmo had found it necessary to change direction in which he was traveling and had decided to accompany the cavalcade of Torreño. There was no doubt in the minds of the others that he was moved by fear of Richard Gidden. But such an opinion could not, of course, be shown. The important thing was to make the celebrated Guadalmo welcome, and for that purpose both the elder and the younger Torreño rode at his side

It was a gloomy day's journey, and at the close of it, when they reached the third rest house of Torreño, built for the comfort and for the honor of Lucia d'Arquista, Don Carlos realized by something in the glance which she cast upon him that the interview had been postponed—not dulled by the delay!

And she had hardly gone to her chambers when one of her serving maids came to him. She wished to see him, and at once. And poor Don Carlos girded up the loins of his resolution and prepared for trouble. It came almost the instant he was before her.

She sat beneath a window of her room with the dust of her journey still upon her clothes, tapping at the big stone flags upon the floor with a tapered riding whip. And while he talked, her glance went continually from the floor to his face to the floor every time she looked at him; he felt as though he had been struck by the lithe body of the whip itself!

"Carlos," she said, "this morning I begged a small favor of you, which was the life of a slave."

He sought his first refuge behind a quibble.

"It was no slave, after all," he said, "but a white man . . . Richard Gidden. I could have saved a hundred, a thousand Indians, Lucia. But this fellow, Gidden . . ."

"What had he done?"

Don Carlos waxed warm with a simulated heat.

"You must remember, Lucia. He invaded my father's house, struck down his servants, took away a guest from his chamber . . ."

"Tush!" said Lucia d'Arquista. "He came for a professional fighter . . . a man who murders according to a legal form . . . Hernandez Guadalmo. He is notorious! He bound two of the servants of that cutthroat. He entered the room of Guadalmo. Did he stab the villain to the heart to avenge the death of his murdered brother? No, no, Carlos. Like a gallant fellow, he took Guadalmo out from the house to a little distance . . . no matter what Guadalmo says, I know the truth, and you have guessed it, too, and so have all the others. He challenged Guadalmo to a fair fight. And before the fight was ended, in came your father's men and saved Guadalmo. That is the only crime against Taki . . . I mean Richard Gidden. I asked that you save this man, Carlos!"

He bit his lip. He was ashamed of his own fear of her.

"Such a man does not need saving," he said with an attempt at lightness. "He saved himself, you see."

"He saved himself from the dogs," said the girl, her anger trembling in her voice now. "Oh, God, that such a thing should be! An honest Christian man hunted with dogs! To be torn to pieces like a wild beast."

"But he was not!" protested Carlos. "He was saved, Lucia. Surely you know that."

"Saved by you?" she asked bitterly.

"Lucia, hear reason . . ."

"I wish to hear much reason. I wish to know, Carlos, why I needed to beg such a favor of you. Why were you not already working with all your might because you loathed such barbarism? Why were you not? Or was it because he had beaten you in a play of foils? Or, in your heart, were you not hungering to see that manhunt?"

When the truth is told about us, it carries with it a sting that pierces through our utmost complacency. Don Carlos had been shaken already. Now he was crimson, and panting as he spoke.

"I could not stir my father. I talked until he was in a furious anger. I could not budge him from his purpose, Lucia!"

"Ah," she said, "if I had been a man, I should have taken my stand at the side of poor Richard Gidden. If the hounds were loosed at him, they should have taken me also!"

He threw out his hands in a gesture of wonder. "After all, he is the Masked Rider . . . He is a highway robber, Lucia. You forget!"

"I forget nothing. What justice could he have in this country except from his own strength? He came here to avenge his brother. He fell into trouble. He was saved by your father . . . by accident, I may say. He went into slavery and took to the highway to repay a debt. Was that not like an honest man? He has repaid the debt. Now he is free to turn his hand to Guadalmo. But you catch him and hunt him with dogs! Ah, it sickens me, Carlos! I only wondered if you would truly try to justify it. And I have heard you."

She turned her back on him and stared out the window. Don Carlos hesitated, turned two or three sentences in his mind, and then decided that the words would not do. He wanted, above all, to have the free blue sky above his head, and he fled at once. He had scarcely left the house when he encountered the last person he wished to meet—his father.

Torreño stopped him. "You have the face of a sick man, Carlos, my son," he said.

"It is nothing," stammered Carlos.

"You are white . . . You are dripping with perspiration. What is it?"

"Nothing," said Carlos.

"Fool!" thundered Torreño. "Will you attempt to hide your thoughts from me?"

The son surrendered on the spot. That ringing voice went through him like a sword.

"It is Lucia," he said faintly. "She is in a fury because of Gidden and the dogs."

"She is in a fury?" repeated Torreño. "She has complained to you?"

Don Carlos sighed and shook his head.

"I shall go to her myself," said Torreño.

Don Carlos caught his arm with an exclamation. "She is not herself . . . She does not know what she says!" he pleaded.

"I shall bring her to herself," said the father roughly, and, shaking himself loose, he went to the door of Lucia's chamber.

She herself opened it to him. He stalked in and threw himself unceremoniously into a chair. She remained standing, looking calmly down at him. Her very calmness enraged him the more. For he loved to inspire fear.

"You have been talking with Carlos," he said sternly.

"He has gone tattling, I see."

"He has answered his father's questions, as a respectful son should."

"I have no doubt, señor, that he is a perfect son."

"You are scornful, Lucia. Now you must understand that in this country, all is not done as it is done in Spain. In a rough land, rough ways are needed."

"I think I understand. Men are hunted instead of boars. Why, señor? Because they are more helpless?"

Torreño writhed in his chair. His voice doubled its volume.

"What I order," he said, smiting his hands together, "is never questioned."

"Do you choose to be obeyed through fear only?" she asked him.

"Obedience is what I demand. The cause of it does not matter."

"Señor, I am as yet a free person. If I marry, I shall swear obedience to your son." And she smiled. The smile maddened Torreño.

"Have a care, girl!" he cried to her. "That marriage has not yet taken place. If you return to Spain unwed . . ."

"You threaten with a sword which has no point, Señor Torreño," she said. "I, also, have been thinking of Spain."

That answer brought Torreño stiffly out of his chair. He stared at her, bewildered. It came suddenly home to him that this was not mere sham—that this girl could indeed contemplate a petty life in old Spain rather than become the queen of the Torreño estate. It staggered him. It shamed him.

"Is that in your brain?" he said. "However, Lucia, you are not a free agent. The marriage has been contracted for. It shall be celebrated if I have to drag you to the altar with my own hands. And when the ceremony is ended, we shall see if you have not two masters instead of one. That is a thing which we shall see!"

He strode to the door and then turned back to her.

"To those who give me obedience, girl," he said, "I am gentle as a lamb. To those who cross me, I am a lion. Lucia, beware!"

With this, he left her, and she heard the beat of his heels and the jingling of his spurs as he went down the corridor.

She went into the next room and found Anna d'Arquista crouched on a bench in the corner with a stricken face.

"You have heard everything?" asked Lucia.

"He spoke so loudly . . ."

"Oh, I am glad that you have heard. That doesn't matter. You see, Aunt Anna, that I have fallen into the hands of hunters. If I cross this frogfaced devil, I suppose that he would set the dogs on me?" She began to laugh savagely, without mirth.

"Lucia, poor child," moaned the spinster, "I have had a foreboding of evil to come. Let us pray to God to bring you happiness in spite of all!"

"It is time to think and to plan," said Lucia. "It is time to remember that I am a d'Arquista. It is time to wish that I were a man!"

XIII

Prudence held some sway in even Francisco Torreño, however, and after supper he walked with the girl in the outer garden where they could hear the steady roar of distant water through a ravine, a sullen noise which seemed to come from the quivering ground beneath their feet.

"Now, Lucia," he said, "while we are alone, and without anger, let us talk over everything and admit that we have made mistakes . . . both of us. I was wrong in treating you as if you were without a brain and a will of your own. You were wrong in saying that you did not wish to marry Carlos. Shall we begin by admitting these things?"

"Señor Torreño," said the girl, "there is no need for sorrow. We have seen the truth about one another. You, señor, have no room on all of your lands for more than one person . . . and that is yourself, of course. I have the same need of room, señor. We could never be happy near one another."

Torreño felt the blind rage swell in his heart. But he controlled himself. He even managed to smile.

"You are still angry," he said. "Young people remain angry

longer than old ones do. Because anger is a childish passion, do you see? But, Lucia, how could your wishes conflict with mine? What is there which we mutually could desire? Will you have rich clothes and many of them? Whatever is made in China or Flanders and all the lands between is yours! Are you fond of jewels? I already have caskets heaped with them . . . trays piled deep as your fingers can clutch! But if you wish more, you shall have more. Are you a lover of hunting! The finest English runners shall be brought half the distance around the world and put in your stables . . . Your stables, Lucia. Do you hear me? Perhaps you love hawking. We have some falcons already. You shall have more! Do you love rich fittings in a house? You may plate your walls with solid gold if you choose! What more is there that a woman can wish? I have known of some bold hearts among your sex who loved the water. Lucia, there are many waterways where the sea is quiet between the islands and the coast. Aye, Lucia, and if you wish to be alone and reign like a queen and never feel any power, you shall have one of those islands . . . the largest . . . for your own. It shall be stocked with cattle and with servants. You shall build a house there according to your will. You shall build ships and trade with them on the seven seas, if you desire.

"You see, child, that when you speak of finding room on my estate, you may have as much as any prince . . . and more! And still, I shall never notice what you have taken."

To this lordly tale, the girl listened with a faint smile.

"There is one rock on which all of those plans would split," she said.

"And that?" asked Torreño.

"Don Carlos."

"Ah? What of him?"

"Which of us would rule him?"

Torreño's face grew dark with angry blood.

"He shall rule himself, señorita."

She waved her hand. "That is folly, señor. I can twist him around my finger, and your very breath makes his whole strong body tremble like a dead leaf. Which would prove the stronger with him? Which of us would he dread the most? Which would he prefer . . . that I should laugh at him or that you should rage at him? I cannot tell. But I feel, señor, that after a time, I should be too strong for you. Therefore, I advise you for your own sake, break off this unhappy marriage."

There was enough of the fox in Torreño to appreciate craft in others. He looked at Lucia with a glint of appreciation in his eyes.

"If I were twenty years younger . . . yes, or ten . . . there would be no question of Carlos. I myself should marry you, Lucia."

"There would be no peace in your house."

"For a year, for two years, no. But after that, I would give you commands by mere glances and liftings of the finger. So! Your voice would never be heard except in answer to my questions. Ah, yes. It would be that way!"

"But since you are too old for this battle, do you think that Carlos has strength for it?"

"I shall teach him," said Torreño. "In the meantime, our grip is on you. You are in our cage. We have thrown the net over your head. Beat your wings, sing your song, but escape if you can, my dear! But you cannot. You belong to me . . . You belong to Carlos. There is the end! In a few months, a few years . . . what is a little time? . . . you will learn to curl up in your nest. All will be well!"

To this she made no answer, but she smiled at him in a way that made his heart fall.

"Tell me, Lucia," he said, "what manner of man could make you love him?"

She answered instantly: "One who could fill me with fear."

"And have you seen such a man in all the world?"

"One."

"And what was he?"

She was silent again, and Torreño stared at her in real bewilderment. But here their interview ended. Filled with a whimsical impulse, he went to Carlos and told him everything, word for word.

"Would you have her under these conditions?"

"I love her," said Carlos sadly. "And if love can breed love, she will come to care for me before the end."

"Bah!" said the elder man. "The mailed fist is the thing for her!"

After that, the great Torreño gave little thought either to his son or to Lucia herself. He had before him what he felt to be more important matters: the details leading to the celebration of the marriage itself, which was to take place within three or four days after their arrival. And so, on the following day, they arrived at Casa Torreño itself.

* * * * *

It was like a child's dream of a castle. Through a shallow little valley, a stream ran and pooled its waters in a spacious lake. Beside the lake was a village of white adobe houses; above the village the road wound to the flat top of a great hill, and on the plateau stood the house itself, built of hewn stone. And at one side, a great square tower arose against the sky.

"Why will you have such a fortress and such a dungeon keep for a house?" asked Lucia.

"So that all the people in the plains may look up to this in clear weather and see the top of the tower . . . You see that it is painted white? And so they know that the eye of their master is on them while they work, while they sleep."

The instant they were in view over the top of the hills, a bell in the great house began to ring, and its larger voice was taken up by the jangle of other bells in the hollow where the village lay. People appeared, streaming from Casa Torreño, and out of the village, a gay-colored procession started up the road. Torreño looked triumphantly toward Lucia, but her face was a blank. The next instant he had broken into curses. For the most inopportune interruption came to break up the solemnity of this occasion. At the last rest house there had been added to his train some couple of fleet greyhounds, and they had been brought along on the leash all day without finding anything to their liking in the way of game. But just at this instant, their sharp voices were raised; Hernandez Guadalmo was heard loudly ordering them to be slipped, and in another instant half a dozen of the lean-bodied hunting dogs were straining across the hills after a flying hare. Behind them rushed Guadalmo and a few others of his immediate train; the followers of Torreño had far too much wit to leave the ranks at such a moment as this.

The diversion took much from the grandeur of the moment, but Hernandez Guadalmo gave no heed to that. He was as greedy a hunter of wild game as he was of man. It mattered not the size of the quarry. The hunt itself was the thing for which he lived. He followed the greyhounds over the first hills and through the next valley. He leaped his horse recklessly across the brook and plunged up the slope beyond, many a length ahead of his closest followers, for nothing they bestrode was comparable with his fine barb. Uphill, however, the hounds gained fast upon him. And the hare fled like a thing possessed of the fiend. It darted up the hill, gaining ground on the dogs at every enormous bound. It reached the more even country beyond, and here the dogs gained at each stride as the hare had gained uphill. And, with each second, the gap between Guadalmo and his men grew greater. He was at the heels of the flying dogs when he saw something stir among the next grove of oaks. A deer, he thought at first. It burst into full view—a bay horse of matchless beauty with flying black mane and tail as it swept toward him, and on its back a tall, familiar figure— Richard Gidden come for the seventh time against him.

The seventh time! If there were any special fate in numbers, one of them must surely fall on this day! And the courage of Guadalmo wavered. There even came into his mind the thought that back yonder among his followers there would be safety—if he turned and fled to them.

But at the thought of flight—and flight before so many witnesses—his soul was steeled to face the ordeal. He caught out a horse pistol from its holster beside the saddle. He brought down the pace of his horse to a hard gallop, and, taking careful aim, he fired at the advancing rider.

But still Gidden closed. There was no gun in the hand of his foe. Only the naked blade of a rapier gleamed in the hand of Gidden as he rushed in. Plainly, he had determined that Guadalmo should die in the same fashion that Gidden's brother had received a death wound from the hand of the Spaniard. He drove straight on at Guadalmo.

It seemed fate, not a mere mortal man, who bestrode that horse. Then Guadalmo threw the pistol away with an oath of fury and snatched out his own rapier. Holding it like a spear at arm's length before him, he spurred the barb at Gidden. They met in half a dozen lightning strides. There was a double flash of light. Then, as Gidden hurtled past and swept off in a great arch away from the Spaniard, Guadalmo threw out his arm, and the sword dropped from his hand.

Still, he held the saddle for a moment with his head thrown back to the sky. He was like a man who sees an enraptured vision. Then he slumped sideways to the ground.

XIV

With song and with dance, with shouting and with music, they brought the cavalcade to Casa Torreño. In all the great house there was only one sad heart, and that was the heart of Lucia d'Arquista. And she, sitting behind her window, looked down across the moonlit valley and saw the bright winding of the creek and the broad silver surface of the lake, darkened at the margin by the shadows of the trees. The air was crisp in these highlands, and a cool breeze blew to her, filled with strange, pungent odors unlike the meadow perfumes of old Spain. All was huge and strong and new in this country at the other end of the world. She was oppressed by its newness; she was oppressed by its size. And for one familiar glimpse of the old land, she would have given ten years of life. Even the singing and the merriment in the house oppressed her more. And her last ally was stolen from her. Anna d'Arquista had been sympathetic enough until she saw the Casa Torreño itself. But after she had walked through it, hall after hall, garden after garden, after she had seen the artificial pools, the statues brought at fearful cost, the stables large and costly as a palace in themselves, her mind was changed.

"There are marriages for love," she had told her niece. "There are also marriages of state. The sons and the daughters of kings submit to them happily enough. Why cannot you, Lucia?"

Lucia made no answer; it was a thing not worth argument, she felt. And the willful blind cannot be made to see.

* * * * *

Torreño himself was quick to see the change in the girl's chaperone. He was at this minute closeted with her. Perhaps he was suggesting certain methods by which she could change the mind of Lucia. As for that, the girl cared nothing. Steel cannot be changed to lead even by magic.

Here the wind increased suddenly almost to a gale—then fell away to its former strength. It was as though a door had been opened and shut behind her. So she turned her head, carelessly. She saw nothing, at first, but just as she was moving back again, the tail of her eye caught on a tall black figure against the wall, half obscured by the curtain. She whipped around upon him. But even before she saw his face, she had no doubt.

"Señor Gidden," she breathed.

"It is I," said the Masked Rider.

"You escaped from Guadalmo's men. I knew that you would! But how by magic did you ever reach this room? They have guards everywhere."

"The same means by which I shall leave it. The hill is tunneled through from top to bottom and steps cut. It was done before the house was built . . . so long ago that even Torreño has forgotten them, I suppose. They brought me up to the cellar level. After that, I have been feeling my way until I reached you."

She was trembling with fear and with delight.

"Where shall I hide you? Where shall I put you, Richard Gidden, madman? They spy on me every step I make. They have listeners at every door!"

"They know that the bird will be out of the cage if they are not wary. But they are cautious too late. She is already gone."

"Señor!" breathed the girl.

"What would you give, señorita, to be free from this house and away on the sea?"

She paused.

"I am paying for every second of this talk," said Gidden a little sternly. "Speak to me as if I were your inner mind. Let there be nothing between us but honesty."

"I would give all my life!" said the girl suddenly. "You knew that or you would never have come. But I am lost. Not even a miracle could save me."

"Yankee hands and Yankee wits will accomplish that miracle," he said. "If you will trust yourself to me. Come to the window."

He led her to the casement.

"Do you see the trees under that hill above the river? I have two horses there . . . my own and a strong black mare which Señor Torreño will miss out of his stable in the morning. They are saddled and bridled. In a few short hours, they will take us to the sea. And in the port there is a Yankee ship loaded and waiting for a fair wind and a word from me. The wind has come. Do you feel it? There is only one thing that keeps the anchor of that skipper down, and that is tidings from Richard Gidden. Will you come with me . . . down those same steps that I climbed to get to you?"

"If we are caught, you are a dead man, señor. I shall not go."

"As well die now as later. They have marked me down. They

are ten thousand to one. Sooner or later they are sure to take me if I stay in this land. Guadalmo's men have sworn to take me!"

"Then flee, Richard Gidden. Ride for the shore and the ship of your friend."

"And leave you here? I cannot! If they were an army, I should stay near you in the hope of seeing you once in a year . . . a single glimpse."

"Do you care so much, Richard?"

"I love you, Lucia."

"And I you, Richard, even when your skin was red and you stood so tall and proud and disdainful before Torreño. I was afraid of you, afraid for you, and I knew that I could love you."

Like two shadows that the wind moved, they swayed together, whispering.

"But I never dreamed that such a wild joy could come to me."

"Now I fear nothing, Lucia. Nothing! I used to think when I sailed for this country that I had only one great purpose in my life, and that was to avenge the death of my poor brother. I was shipwrecked and lived among Indians. I felt that God kept me for that end alone. I was hunted for my life. And still I felt something predestined that would bring me on. But it was not to meet Guadalmo. It was to find you, my dear, and save you from the calf, Don Carlos, and the bull, his father. Save you and keep you and love you forever."

"Richard, if . . ."

A footfall in the hall.

She started back from him. "It is my aunt!"

"It cannot be."

The footfall approached, paused at the door, and then went on.

"Now," he said, "that is a warning. Are you ready?"

"One instant. My jewels, Richard . . ."

"Let them be. Let them be. I am robbing Torreño of you. Let him keep the jewels. They will be a part repayment. I want you as you are, my dear. Without a thing, without a penny. To be all mine!"

"If they see us as we go . . . if you are lost, Richard . . . I want to carry some weapon. They shall not have me back!"

"Hush, my dear. That is a sin. No harm shall come. Are you quite ready?"

"Yes."

"Is there one regret?"

"None in all the world!"

XV

They slipped into the outer corridor. A door opened; a shaft, a soft yellow lamplight slipped down the wall. But the footsteps which sounded immediately went before them, almost as though leading the way. And the lovers looked at one another with suffused faces, with glistening eyes, thinking the same thought.

Now down the hall to the rear of the house. They reached a stairway at the back, narrow, swiftly turning, and down this Richard Gidden descended first, with Lucia behind him, and as he climbed down, he could feel the tremor of her breath behind him and sometimes catch a whispered word, so he knew that she was praying for their safety. But he needed no prayers to help him. He felt the strength of a lion in him.

They turned a sharp corner of the stairs—a servant, scampering up, crashed against Gidden and recoiled, staggering.

"In the name of heaven," he gasped out.

"Dog!" said Gidden sternly. "Are you a blind bat?"

The magnificence of his manner struck the other full of awe. He cowered against the wall.

"Alas, señor, on these steps . . . the servants only . . . I did not know . . ."

Gidden brushed past him with Lucia on his arm.

"He has stopped and is staring after us. He begins to suspect something," said Gidden. "The devil fly away with him. I should have stabbed him to the heart and gone on without a word."

"No, no, Richard, only when your own life is in danger . . . swear that you will not harm a single human soul! If there is blood on this first day . . ."

"The devil is loose!" murmured Gidden. "He has given an alarm. Did you have the hood over your face?"

There was a loud babbling of voices from the rear of the great house.

"I had the hood over it. He could not have guessed."

"He has guessed, nevertheless, Lucia. We can never reach the bottom of the hill by the hidden stairs before the whole household will be swarming like hornets."

"We are lost, then, Richard? Shall I turn back? Shall I hide you?"

"You could not hide me here if I were no larger than a grain of sand. Old Torreño would smell me out. Keep heart, Lucia. We walk straight forward and trust to blind chance."

They entered the great hall. Yonder sat Don Carlos himself at a small table with a book in his hand, but with idle, sad eyes fixed straight before him.

"We are lost," whispered the girl.

"Not yet. He knows my red face, not my white one. And you are hooded. He will think it strange, but he is in a dream. Perhaps he will not even see. We must walk straight toward the big door, yonder. If I have to delay, run straight forward, my dear. There are horses in the courtyard tethered at the rack.

Take one, and ride with all speed down the hill. I shall be after you in a trice . . . or else I shall be a dead man. Do you hear?"

"Yes!"

"And are you afraid?"

"No!"

"Then . . ."

"Señor, señor!" broke in the voice of Don Carlos from the side.

"Señor Torreño," said Gidden in his perfect Spanish and with a courteous intonation. To the girl: "Faster, my dear!"

"One moment!"

"On, on," whispered Gidden. "I must stop here for an instant. Show no haste. Be slow and at ease. Sing a song softly. It will be better than a mask!"

He turned to Carlos.

"I have not your face in my mind, señor," said the young Torreño. "Are you one of poor Don Hernandez's men?"

"I am, señor," said Gidden.

"Your name, then?"

"Christobal Paraña."

"Paraña? I have heard all the names of his men. I do not recall that one. Yet there is something familiar about your face. It is connected with some sinister recollection in my mind, sir."

"I shall explain to you whatever you wish when I return. The girl . . ."

He gestured.

"Señor!" said Carlos sternly. "Stand where you are. I have the strangest thought in the world. You are Gidden!"

He was drawing his pistol as he spoke. Half of its silver-chased length was in view when Gidden caught his wrist with fingers of hot steel that crushed the flesh against the bone and made him drop the weapon. He himself tore the pistol out and with the heavy barrel of it struck poor Don Carlos to the floor and that in the view of half a dozen mozos. The servants raised a shout. Someone fired a gun.

But Gidden was already out of the hall and down the white stone steps into the courtyard. There he saw Lucia mounted on a tall gelding, with the reins of another in her hand. Before her stood a cavalier of Guadalmo's troop, half frowning, half smiling. No doubt it was his very horse, by unlucky chance, that she had mounted.

He saw before him greater obstacles. There were a dozen armed men in that court. Two watched the gate steadfastly. Others were scattered here and there. It was plain that Torreño considered his house a garrisoned fort until that marriage was consummated.

"Don Carlos!" shouted Gidden as he raced out. "They are murdering Don Carlos! Help!"

That startling word brought a rush from the nearest men to the door, and there they crushed against the outcoming tide of those in pursuit of Gidden. Only one man had stayed by his place, and that was he who argued with Lucia. Gidden bounded on him like a tiger and struck him to the ground, then leaped into the saddle of the horse which Lucia held. He had one glimpse of her pale, set face, then they whirled and raced for the gateway.

Through that gateway they pressed at full speed and, out of the babble swelling confusedly behind them, they heard one great single voice—the voice of Don Carlos: "It is Gidden and the Señorita Lucia! Kill the man."

A gun exploded, but it must have been fired wildly, for not even the sound of the bullet came to them. Then they were rushing down the looping road which led to the base of the hill. Halfway down they looked back to Casa Torreño's

stone face, pale in the moonlight, and a dark tangle of horsemen who spurred out from the gate. Then, face forward, they
goaded their horses and galloped for the stream. The stone
bridge rang beneath the heavy hoofs. They tore up the valley
toward that shadow of trees beneath the hills where the picked
horses of Gidden waited for them.

Twenty riders stormed behind them, and the leaders were
gaining when Gidden and Lucia reached the covert. It seemed
the ropes which tied the horses were strands of iron, refusing to
be loosed. And the horses themselves were possessed of devils,
dancing wildly, unwilling to be mounted. By sheer might of
hand, he raised the girl and put her into the saddle. Then into
the saddle on the back of the bay Gidden leaped. The brush
was already crashing with the charge of Torreño's men as they
started away on their fresh mounts.

They issued on the farther side. Through the trees, shadows
among shadows, the horsemen of Torreño cursed and spurred
and shouted. Don Carlos, pressing toward the front, was offering thousands and fresh thousands for the capture.

But the fugitives had beneath them, now, speed like the
gallop of the wind. A long level lay before them, twisting
around the shoulders of hills which stepped down into the
valley, and over it they raced, with the clamor growing fainter
behind them.

* * * * *

It was a black sea under the cold light of dawn that they saw
at last. But rocking on the waters of the little harbor, they saw
the long body of a ship. To them it was like a promised land.
On the hilltop above the beach, they loosed the two horses.
The black mare raced off with high head and flaring tail, but

the bay horse followed his master curiously and watched as the pair with numbed, weary hands, gathered driftwood and kindled two fires.

"If they come . . . if Torreño comes before the boat?" she breathed, as they stood shivering beside the growing fires.

"Fate," said Gidden, "is against them. Look!"

From the side of the ship, a boat had put off and was heading to the shore, swinging on with the rhythmic stroke of half a dozen men. It came closer. In the sheets stood a tall man, waving his hat, calling, and they hurried down to the edge of the water, where the wet sands yielded beneath their feet.

The bow cut the sand. The sailors leaped out, regardless of the icy water, but Gidden was already waist deep beside the gunwale, bearing the girl in his arms. And as she was lowered gently to a place, she heard a man in the bow saying in the unfamiliar English tongue: "Dick Gidden, we have cheated the devil and got you safe! But here are two birds instead of one!"

"It is the spring of the year," said Gidden.

THE END

ABOUT THE AUTHOR

Max Brand® is the best-known pen name of Frederick Faust, creator of Dr. Kildare, Destry, and many other fictional characters popular with readers and viewers worldwide. His enormous output, totaling approximately thirty million words or the equivalent of five hundred and thirty ordinary books, covered nearly every field: crime, fantasy, historical romance, espionage, Westerns, science fiction, adventure, animal stories, love, war, and fashionable society. Eighty motion pictures have been based on his works, along with many radio and television programs. Perhaps no other author has reached more people in such a variety of different ways. Born in Seattle in 1892, orphaned early, Faust grew up in the rural San Joaquin Valley of California. At Berkeley he became a student rebel and one-man literary movement, contributing prodigiously to all campus publications. Denied a degree because of unconventional conduct, he embarked on a series of adventures culminating in New York City where, after a period of near starvation, he received simultaneous recognition as a serious poet and successful author of fiction. Later, he traveled widely, making his home in New York, then in Florence, Italy, and finally in Los Angeles. Once the United States entered the Second World War, Faust abandoned his lucrative writing career and his work as a screenwriter to serve as a war correspondent with the infantry in Italy, despite his fifty-one years and a bad heart. He was killed during a night attack on a hilltop village held by the German army. New books based on magazine serials or unpublished manuscripts or restored versions continue to appear so that, alive or dead, he has averaged a new book every six months for seventy-five years. Beyond this, some work by him is newly reprinted every week of every year in one or another format somewhere in the world. A great deal more about this author and his work can be found in *The Max Brand Companion* (Greenwood Press, 1997) edited by Jon Tuska and Vicki Piekarski.